For Rett,
I hope you like these games from the past. Enjoy!
Kay S. Heath

Ida Claire, It's Summertime!

Ninth Printing

Kay Strickland Heath

Ida Claire, It's Summertime!

Kay Strickland Heath

To order additional copies of her books, or to discuss speaking engagements, please contact the author directly:
Kay S. Heath
(229) 894-1711
Email: kayheath@mchsi.com

PUBLISHED BY:
BRENTWOOD ACADEMIC PRESS
POST OFFICE BOX 4773
COLUMBUS, GEORGIA 31914-4773
(800) 334-8861

Introduction

School is out! Summer is finally here! Will is excited because that means Ida Claire will be home all day long every day. He tells about all the things they find to do daily. Sometimes these adventures are funny. Sometimes they are scary.

Will already knows how to play lots of games like marbles, tag, and hopscotch. But, he learns more about many other things like rock school, rope mountain climbing, sling the statue, and fireworks!

Will knows when school starts back, he will be going for the first time. He sometimes gets a little worried about it. But, Ida Claire and Will stay busy - having fun!

Dedication

For Leann,
who always enjoys listening to my childhood stories, and
for Leon and Mike,
the true Franklin and Will!

Acknowledgements

There are many people I want to acknowledge that have affected the outcome of this manuscript. First I want to express gratitude to my wonderful parents. I am fortunate to have been raised in a happy, loving, and caring home. My parents continue to be very supportive of any goal I strive to attain. They are two of the first that heard about Ida Claire's and Will's adventures. Together we can recall the many fond memories. Thank you, Mama and Daddy, for all your love and support.

I want to thank my husband. He has always encouraged me to strive to reach my goals. In his patient and quiet manner he urges me to be myself and grow. Thank you, Johnny. A special thanks to our wonderful daughter, Leann. She continues to be a joy daily. The story in the book about the rabbit is her story. Thank you, Leann, for allowing me to share it with others.

There are many teachers that had an impact on my life. I want to thank all of them. However, four of these truly affected my future. These are Jane Lee, Martha Spurlock, Laura West, and Jean Lark. During their teaching careers, these ladies demonstrated their concern for each student. All were willing for students to see their human side through sharing their humor and feelings with students. Their caring impressed me and set a wonderful example for me to follow as a teacher. Each of these teachers became my mentor and friend.

These acknowledgements would not be complete without a special expression of gratitude to my closest friend, Gail Rowell. Her confidence in me motivated me to write this book. She never seemed to doubt my ability to accomplish it. And, inadvertently, she is responsible for the name Ida Claire!

Contents

Chapter 1

Wonders Never Cease

Three days before yesterday, my cousin, Ida Claire, came over early one morning and wanted to know what we could play that would be fun. She really could have asked what "adventure" was I ready to attempt because with Ida Claire any playtime was an adventure. We were lucky. We lived next to each other. We were kin and we were best friends. Ida Claire Loudly's Mama was my Aunt Ima. But, my last name was Lee. The fact that our Mamas were sisters made us first cousins. Anyway, back to our adventure for the day.

We considered cardboard box house building, playing marbles, or climbing in the mimosa tree. But we decided jumping off the porch would be the best thing to do for that particular day. Now this porch was not just any old low, house porch. This particular porch ran the entire width of the Rotary Clubhouse building. It took about thirty-five running steps from one end to the other. I was gonna be in first grade after summertime, and I had learned to count. I didn't have to go to kindergarten either because Ida Claire was my teacher when we played school. I knew she was smart because she had finished second grade last year.

This porch on the clubhouse was high off the ground. It had seven steps up to it. As a matter of fact, when I stood on the ground right next to it, it was a little bit taller than me. Anyway, we asked Aunt Ima if we could go up to the clubhouse porch. We didn't have to cross any streets because it was on the same block. Aunt Ima told us that it would be okay just as long as we didn't get in the street and didn't do any jumping. We didn't really talk about it, but both of us knew that a porch like the clubhouse porch was a mighty fine jumping place. But Aunt Ima was the type that meant she was boss and she believed that children, especially hers, had better mind her.

Well, we got to the porch. It was shaded and nice and cold. It had a wide roof on it and was made of concrete. Your legs could always get cooled off if you sat down and stretched them out. Both of us had on shorts and were barefooted. That porch felt nice and cold to our feet, too. It felt especially cold since we had run on the hot, sunny sidewalk to get to the clubhouse.

We played for a little while hunting roly-poly bugs on the shaded ground at one end of the porch. At this same end of the porch we noticed that the grass and clover hadn't been cut. It looked thick and green and soft. Ida Claire said to me, "Will, I don't think that Mama can see us from the house, do you?" I didn't really have to think about it because Ida Claire was smart, and I knew she had already figured out that question before she asked me. I also knew that the "adventure" was about to begin. She grinned and said, "I'll jump if you will!" So we both ran around the corner of the porch and up the front steps. It was too tall for us to climb on that end of the porch anyway. Even though I was younger and a boy, Ida Claire said that the first time we would jump together. We always tried to be fair. So we grabbed each other's hands and ran out to the end of the porch and shouted, "Jump!" We did! We landed in the soft clover and got up as quickly as we could. We ran around the corner and back up the steps and grabbed each other's hands again and went sailing through the air to the soft clover. I'm not sure how many times we repeated this. But we did it enough that Ida Claire finally decided to change the game. So, then it became a contest of seeing who could jump the farthest.

We took turns. We thought if we could start running a little farther back on the porch, then we could jump out farther away from the porch. We never did determine who had jumped the farthest. But, I reckon it crossed Ida Claire's mind that Aunt Ima had told us not to be doing any jumping. When she remembered that, she said, "Will, you jump one more time and then I'll jump one more time." That's when I came to realize that there's such a thing as "pressing your luck". My jump went fine. Ida Claire started her run on the porch way back at the other end. Those extra steps at the beginning must have paid off because she went sailing through the air and went longer out from the porch than on any other jump. As a matter of fact, she landed in a completely new spot of tall, thick clover. As a matter of fact, the clover and grass were so thick neither one of us could see the broken bottle that was in it. Now, Ida Claire was a pretty good jumper but her landing wasn't the best. She always landed on her knees and elbows. And her right elbow landed on the broken bottle. She screamed and looked up at me. And, shoot, I didn't know what to do. But, when I saw all that blood, I was mighty scared. We started walking back towards the house and Ida Claire was holding her elbow. The blood was trickling down her arm and dripping off her little finger. I just kept bouncing up and down going around Ida Claire. I kept asking her what she wanted me to do. She wasn't really crying but she looked scared. I asked her if it hurt and she said not as much as her seat would for not minding her Mama. I knew that was the truth for sure because nobody crossed Aunt Ima. I told Ida Claire, "I reckon you'll get a bad whipping!"

She said quietly, "I reckon so." The blood kept dripping on the hot sidewalk and it left a trail. The closer we got to the house the more Ida Claire started to sob. By the time we got to the back door, tears were streaming down her face. I didn't know if her elbow was hurting more or she was getting more scared about her whipping from Aunt Ima.

I had heard somebody say one time, "Wonders never cease." I found out right then exactly what that meant. Aunt Ima looked at Ida Claire and said, "Well, let me look at how bad you're really hurt. I'll have to wash it good first." So Ida Claire had to put her arm in the sink for Aunt Ima to wash it off and look at it. Aunt Ima got the tweezers and pulled the little pieces of glass out of the cut. Then, very carefully, she wrapped Ida Claire's elbow with a gauze bandage. She tore an old sheet and made her a sling for her right arm. And Ida Claire wore that neat sling for the rest of the day. It made me wish that I had been the one to make the longest jump. Wonders never cease!

Chapter 2

To Bee Or Not To Bee

Three days after Ida Claire quit wearing her sling to hold up her injured elbow, she came over to my house. She showed me the BandAid over her cut. She said that Aunt Ima thought she should have taken her to Dr. Kneed. He probably would have put some stitches in it so it wouldn't become an ugly scar. Ida Claire thought that the stitches might have hurt. So she was glad that her Mama didn't think of going to the doctor the day that she got hurt. Anyway, Ida Claire wanted to know if I wanted to play anything. Shoot! I was always ready for any adventure with Ida Claire. She said that Franklin, her big brother, had an idea of something we could do.

Franklin was five years older than Ida Claire. He was in seventh grade last year. He called us "Squirts" and usually didn't want to play with us. But, sometimes, when he didn't have anything else to do; or, I should say, when he couldn't find his buddies to hang around with, then he'd boss me and Ida Claire. But we didn't mind too much. We were just glad to have a new adventure. Franklin would come up with super neat ideas usually. And my Mama and Aunt Ima didn't worry about us if Franklin was there to watch over us!

Franklin told us to get a quart size jar with a screw-type lid and meet him at the mimosa tree. We all loved the mimosa tree in the summertime. It always had the nicest green fern type leaves that made great shade. It was great for climbing, too. Its trunk and big branches were close to the ground and the limbs forked out to make a good place for sitting up in the cool shaded tree. It was pretty to look at too because of its pink flowers. The flowers looked sorta like pink starbursts. Sometimes Ida Claire would pick one and put it in her hair. She thought it looked real pretty that way. Yep, we loved the mimosa tree in the front yard. But we weren't the only ones that loved it. Big black and yellow bumblebees loved it, too. They would zoom in and bury themselves in the pink flowers for a minute, then buzz out to another pink flower to stay for another minute. Franklin said that they were pollinating. He sure was smart. But, we didn't tell him that because he would really get the big head then. Anytime we played in the mimosa tree Aunt Ima told us to be careful because if those bees stung us, it would really hurt!

Franklin decided that today was a good day to get rid of some of those buzzing bumblebees. He took the jar in his right hand and the lid in his left hand. He told us to watch. Shoot, mine and Ida Claire's eyes were glued to that jar and Franklin. He waited until he saw a bee go into one of the pink flowers. Then he reached out and closed that lid over the jar right on top of the flower, surrounding the bee and scooping it into the jar. He let out a "Hooray!" We clapped and squealed. Franklin said, "That's one. Now, for the next one." Ida Claire and I looked at each other. She started to go get another jar. Franklin stopped her and told her that she didn't have to do that. All she had to do was watch him. He shook the jar really hard with both hands and stopped the shaking. He acted like he was going to throw the jar down. The flower and the bee were at the bottom of the jar then. So, Franklin got real close to another pink flower. He saw the bee go into it. Very quickly he unscrewed the lid and snatched the flower with the bee in it, into the jar and put the lid back on tight. Now he had two flowers AND two bees. This time he said, "Yeah!" And we just clapped and squealed again. He caught seventeen bees in that same jar. We counted out loud, clapped, and squealed for each one. Ida Claire told me that this was a good way to practice counting my numbers. I thought she was right because it was really fun this way!

Ida Claire said, "Will, just listen to those bees. When they're on the outside, their buzzing sounds loud and noisy. But, inside that jar, those bees just sound like they're humming." We all laughed at that. Then she said to Franklin, "Seems to me like when you take that lid off to let them go, you are gonna have some mighty mad bees. And they might sting us bad like Mama said."

Franklin looked at Ida Claire and said, "Are you crazy? We're going to take care of these bees so they won't sting anybody. Go get me the ice pick." Ida Claire looked at me wondering if I knew what Franklin was planning. Shoot, I sure didn't have any idea, but I couldn't wait to find out!

We went in to ask Aunt Ima for the ice pick. She told me on the way to the house that Aunt Ima might not let her have it because it could be dangerous. You could poke somebody's eyes out if you weren't careful. So she went into the house saying, "Mama, Franklin says that he needs to use the ice pick for a minute." She knew that Aunt Ima would probably let her have it if she was getting it for Franklin. Aunt Ima was busy ironing. Just as Ida Claire got to the drawer where the ice pick was kept, Aunt Ima asked, "What in the world does he want with that ice pick?" Ida Claire said that she didn't know. So, she wasn't telling a story to Aunt Ima. Aunt Ima told both of us to be careful because it could be dangerous.

When we got back to Franklin, he asked us, "What took y'all so long? I had time to catch four more of those bees while y'all were in the house." Shoot, that made twenty-one in that jar now. Ida Claire asked him what he was going to do with the ice pick. Franklin said, "Y'all just watch. A bee that's drowned can't sting anybody." I just looked at Ida Claire and she looked at me and we both shrugged our shoulders. He finally told us that he would poke some holes in the jar lid, then put the jar with the holes in the lid up under the water spigot. When the water went into the jar, that would drown those bees. And they would never sting us. Franklin sure was smart.

He grabbed around the edge of the jar with his left hand. His first finger and thumb went almost halfway around that lid. Then, with the ice pick in his right hand, he started to jab the lid in the center. He told us, "You, Squirts, don't get too close. I don't want to poke out your eyes!" When he said that, I blinked for the first time since he started jabbing the holes. I looked at Ida Claire and she grinned. I didn't know how many holes it would take. But I was glad when Franklin said, "One more ought to be just fine." But about the time he got the word "fine" out of his mouth, something happened that wasn't so fine. He jabbed that ice pick into his hand. It went right in the stretchy skin part between the finger and the thumb. Franklin gritted his teeth, but he didn't cry. Ida Claire asked him if it hurt. He said, "Naw, Stupid, it feels just great." Ida Claire had turned sorta white and pale-looking. I just started jumping up and down and going around Franklin asking him, "What are we gonna do? What are we gonna do?" Franklin kept gritting his teeth, but he said, "We gotta go show Mama." When Aunt Ima saw the three of us come in, she turned off the iron and sat down in the nearest chair. She saw the wooden part of the ice pick on the top of Franklin's hand and the metal sharp point sticking out under his hand. She said, "What in the world?!?" She told Ida Claire and me to go back to my house and tell my Mama what had happened.

It seemed like a really long time before Aunt Ima and Franklin came back from Dr. Kneed's office. I felt sorta sick every time I thought about the way that ice pick looked. When they came back from the doctor, Franklin and Aunt Ima came to our house. He said that Dr. Kneed poured some stinking stuff on the spot, then just yanked the ice pick out. He didn't even have to have any stitches. After he left, Ida Claire told me that Franklin was really a brave person. She said that he was courageous, too. She had learned that big word last year in second grade. I could tell that she was proud to have a big brother like Franklin. Shoot, I was even proud that he was my cousin.

Chapter 3

Seeing Is Believing

Three days later early in the morning it started raining. I asked Mama if I could go see what Ida Claire was doing. She said, "That will be fine - just don't get too wet." When I got to Ida Claire's house, she was playing solitaire with a deck of cards. We both loved to play cards. We played a game of War, then Slap-Jack. We even played a hand of Canasta. Just as soon as I knew what numbers looked like, my big sister Hannah taught Franklin, Ida Claire, and me how to play all kinds of card games. We played partners and she had to help me a lot, but we were learning together. Hannah went off to college in Atlanta. She was in high school when I was born; so, she was a lot older. She told me and Ida Claire that it took a lot of practice to be a good card player. Shoot! Hannah must have practiced every day because she sure was good.

We could tell by the smell that Aunt Ima was cooking something good in the kitchen. I asked Ida Claire if she thought it was about time for dinner. She said, "Yeah, Will, it is just about time for dinner, but last year my teacher, Mrs. Taylor, said that it could be called lunch." I didn't care what anybody called it. I just knew that my stomach was gnawing and I was mighty hungry. We had eating time worked out pretty good. If I was at Ida Claire's during dinnertime, we ate over at her house. And if she was at my house when Mama was through cooking, we ate at my house. It didn't matter to us because Aunt Ima and Mama both could really cook good stuff. Today we had fried chicken, brown butterbeans, mashed potatoes, sliced tomatoes, fried cornbread, and good, cold tea. Ida Claire and I both loved to mix up all our vegetables together on the plate. The mashed potatoes were usually at the bottom, then we piled up the brown butterbeans and bits of tomato on top. We also smashed up the cornbread into the pile. It might not have looked too good to Aunt Ima, but she never did fuss about it. It didn't matter how it looked because it tasted great. Ida Claire did tell me that I wouldn't be able to mix up my food good like that when I started to school. She said, "But it won't matter too much though because the food is not as good anyway." While Aunt Ima was cleaning up the kitchen, we finished our card game. Since it was raining outside and we couldn't go play outdoors, we wondered what we could do. Ida Claire slapped her leg and said, "I know--we'll get Mama to tell us a story about the good old days." She ran into the kitchen and said, "Mama, will you tell us about when you were a little girl just about my age?"

Aunt Ima said, "Yeah, y'all younguns are sights always wanting to hear stories about olden times." So Ida Claire and I climbed up on the couch and we both sat crosslegged like an Indian ready to hear about Aunt Ima when she was a little girl. Aunt Ima came into the living room wiping her hands with a dish towel. She plopped down in her favorite chair and blew out a sigh. Ida Claire propped her elbows on her knees and then put her hands on the side of her jaws. That looked pretty comfortable; so I tried it too. We both were ready to hear Aunt Ima's story about the olden days. Anytime Aunt Ima told us a story, it seemed like it was really happening. The good thing about it was no matter how scared we were, we were able to look at each other and know that we were safe right in Ida Claire's living room. Aunt Ima cleared her throat and the story adventure began:

"Well, when I was a little girl about your age, Ida Claire, we lived out in the country on a farm. The house we lived in was on the old Mays' place. My Mama, brother, big sister, (that would be your mama, Will) and Grandpa were out in the field picking cotton. It was a hot summer day. And they were all tired and sweaty. They had gotten mighty thirsty out there and Mama called for me to come out to the field. My cousin Lucille and I were playing in the backyard. Lucille was two years older, but she didn't have to pick cotton either."

Ida Claire asked, "Why didn't you and Lucille have to pick cotton?" Aunt Ima told us that she and Lucille weren't old enough. But she also said that it was her job to go get water for the ones in the field that needed it. Then she continued telling her story.

"So I heard Mama calling, and we ran to the field to see what she wanted. She told me to go back to the well and get them a bucket full of water. She reminded me to be sure and not bust the bottom out of the bucket by dropping it down too fast or by letting go of the crank. The way you were supposed to get the water up from the bottom of the well was to turn the crank pulley and lower the bucket on the pulley down to the bottom, then turn the crank the other way and bring it up. Anyway, I had to stand on my tiptoes but I could bring up a bucket almost full of water. We got to the well and started lowering the bucket. The well was in the back corner of the yard, but I felt like someone was looking at me from the house. Sure enough, I looked up and on the back porch I saw a woman standing there. She had on a long-sleeved, light-colored dress. Now, I knew that all of the grown-ups of the house were supposed to be in the cotton field except my Granny. But this woman was taller than my Granny. And usually Granny wore dark colors. I asked Lucille if she knew who that woman was. She told me that she didn't. We were a little too far to see her face real good, but I called to her, "Granny." She didn't answer. So I hollered a little louder, "GRANNY!" A voice from down the road said, "What is it, Honey?" I recognized Granny's voice. But, she was answering me from the porch of a neighbor's house down the road. We knew then that that woman on the porch wasn't Granny. Lucille and I looked at each other; then we looked back at the porch. But, it was empty! The woman had disappeared! Lucille and I decided to go see where she went. I pulled the well bucket up and sat it on the side of the well. As we started going towards the house, we heard a rattling sound like chains being drug around the dining room table. I told Lucille that I knew exactly who it was now. Probably Uncle Ferris was up to his foolishness. He always liked to play a joke on somebody, and he had probably dressed up like an old woman to scare us. And he was probably making that noise in the dining room, too. Uncle Ferris was my Mama's little brother, and he would do anything for a laugh. Lucille agreed with me. It had to be Uncle Ferris.

We decided to go check it out and show him that he hadn't scared us. The closer we got to the dining room, the louder we could hear the rattling sounds. So, we started walking quietly on our tiptoes until we got to the side window. We both slowly edged up to the window and peeked in, but as soon as we did, the noise stopped completely! And nothing was moving or even IN the room. We didn't see Uncle Ferris or anybody. We ran back to the well. It seemed like a good idea to put some distance between us and the house. When we got back to the well, I told Lucille that we better get that water to the folks in the field. I started lowering the bucket again and all of a sudden we heard that rattling sound again. When we looked up, that old woman was back on the porch. She had her arms reaching out towards us! I told Lucille that I might get a whipping, but I turned loose that crank, and both of us took out running to the field. I pulled my sunhat down over one side of my face (the side that was facing the old woman). I was out of breath by the time I got to Mama, but I told her as quickly as I could everything that had happened. Grandpa had stopped picking cotton and was standing there listening. When I got through explaining, he said, 'Yep, that old woman is Old Lady Mays!' My Mama said to him, 'Now, Papa, don't say that, you'll scare the younguns!' I asked her why that would scare us. My Mama didn't say anything. But, Grandpa said, "Because Old Lady Mays died twenty years ago!' I asked Grandpa if he believed in ghosts - and he said to me, 'Well, seeing is believing!' Then Aunt Ima said, "And that's just one of the strange things I remember from living in the house on the old Mays' place." Aunt Ima was through telling her story!

I looked over at Ida Claire and she was biting her fingernails. I swallowed hard and asked Aunt Ima if that story really did happen. And she said, "It sure did. As a matter of fact, that old house is still standing. I'll take y'all younguns out there to see it sometimes!" Ida Claire asked her Mama exactly where was that house. Aunt Ima said, "Oh, it's about eight miles out in the country." Ida Claire and I both felt relieved. We were mighty glad that old Mays' house wasn't too close to where we lived now!

Chapter 4

Cowboys, Clay, And What Grown-ups Say

Three balls of modeling clay were the only ones I could find when I looked in the bottom of my toy chest the next day. I had the yellow, red, and blue clay, but I couldn't find the green and brown. Ida Claire had made the brown by mixing a little bit of all the others together. I knew Ida Claire would be able to find the other two balls. She could always dig around in my toy chest and find stuff that I thought was lost for sure. I asked Mama if I could call Ida Claire and ask her about it. We hadn't had our telephone for very long and I was supposed to always ask Mama about it if I wanted to use it. She thought that you shouldn't use that new-fangled thing too much because you might wear it out. But, she told me that it would be okay to call Ida Claire. I picked up the talking-into part of the phone and put the other end up to my ear. A lady said, "Number, please?" I told her the number 425. That was the way for me to get Ida Claire's house. The phone made a ringing sound.

Ida Claire said, "Hello." I asked her if she could come help me find the other modeling clay so we could make something. She said, "I'll be right there, Will." While I was waiting on Ida Claire, I thought about that I didn't know my own phone number by heart like I knew Ida Claire's. I asked Mama about that.

She said, "That's normal, Will, I'm the same way. We don't ever have to call our own number but we call over at your Aunt Ima's house more that anywhere else." About the only other time that Mama used the phone, besides to talk to Hannah, was when she called Mr. Sims to give him her grocery list. Mr. Sims' grocery store was down the street, and he would deliver the groceries in his green truck to folks' houses. Mama ordered her groceries like that because she couldn't drive. So if Daddy was gone on the road for his job, she couldn't get to the grocery store unless she asked Aunt Ima to take her.

"Did you look way down in the bottom in the back of the toy chest, Will?" Ida Claire asked me as she came in the back door. She stuck out her foot and caught the back door just before it slammed shut. That screened door could make quite a racket if you just let it shut by itself. I told her that I thought the other two balls of modeling clay must be lost for sure. We both went to my bedroom and started digging into the toy chest. The first thing that Ida Claire pulled out was my black cowboy holster set with silver guns. She said that we might could play "cowboys" after we got through playing with the modeling clay. I thought that was a pretty good idea. We both kept digging through puzzles, gloves, puppets, and marbles. Then we found another cowboy holster. This one was red and the guns in it had white pearl handles. Yep, we would definitely play "cowboys" just as soon as we finished playing with the clay. Ida Claire looked in the back and said, "I think I see those other two balls, Will." So she pulled them out, and we both started taking out the little plastic cowboys and Indian men. We found the plastic horses, the corral fencing, and the Indian teepees, too. We hauled all of them to the kitchen table. The table in the kitchen had a green, slick, and shiny Formica top. It had chrome all around the edges. It made a mighty nice bottom to whatever we decided to make with the modeling clay. We asked Mama for a knife we could use to get out Western town fixed. We wanted the store fronts nice and smooth. She gave us a round-ended knife so nobody could get hurt. It was a lot like Matt Dillon's Dodge City on "Gunsmoke". We had watched that show on TV last week. Of course, we let the Indians come into our town, too. We had horses in the corral and a saloon for Miss Kitty. But, since we didn't have a plastic lady figure, we just made-like that she was in the saloon and nobody could see her. We had a shoot-out between the Indians and the cowboys. They kept getting shot off their horses and kept falling off left and right. Sometimes we would make one do a double flip and then we would rare back, up on our knees in the chairs, and just giggle and laugh out loud.

We were just as busy playing with our little men as we could be. About that time Aunt Ima came in the back door. Mama asked her if she wanted a cup of coffee. She said that that sounded mighty good to her. Mama told us that we'd used her kitchen table long enough and that we needed to start cleaning up the toys and putting them back where they belonged. Ida Claire started scraping up the modeling clay with the knife. That shiny tabletop didn't look too shiny anymore. I started stuffing the little men and horses into my shorts' pockets because I couldn't carry them all in my hands. Ida Claire got busy rolling the modeling clay up in the right color ball. She didn't want to mix anymore, so when she finished, she had five balls. We both ran into my room to put all of the things we had back in the toy chest. We heard Aunt Ima say, "Did you hear what happened to Jesse?" Mama said that she didn't. I started to ask Ida Claire what she wanted to play next. But she motioned to me with the quiet sign to not talk. I knew that when Ida Claire put that pointing finger up to her closed tight lips that I better hush in a hurry. We tiptoed closer to the kitchen door so we could hear exactly what did happen to Jesse. We knew Jesse. He was a grown man and he was a cousin to Aunt Ima and Mama. It depended on which grown-up that was talking to know exactly what Jesse's problem was. Our Grandmama was sweet and didn't say anything bad about anybody. She just said that Jesse had a little problem, and it sure was bad on his family. Hannah said that he was an alcoholic. But she went to college and always used big words. Aunt Ima said that he was a drunk. And Ida Claire's Daddy, Uncle Ben, said that Jesse was just a plain "sot".

We heard Aunt Ima say, "Well, Jesse had been doing pretty good and hadn't touched a drop for almost a month. Then, his old army buddy, Lester, came to the house. He had some "shine" in his trunk. Well, that was "Katie barred the door"! I looked at Ida Claire. I had gotten lost with Aunt Ima's talk. She liked to use words that she called "old sayings". I didn't know who Katie was, and I sure didn't know what a shiny trunk had to do with anything.

Ida Claire whispered for us to go into the kitchen and get some water and act like we didn't hear a thing. We had learned that if you ask something when the grown-ups are talking, then they won't talk if you are anywhere around. I didn't know what all the fuss was about. A few weeks back Aunt Ima was telling my Mama that Shelia was "expecting" and would be marrying Lenny pretty soon. When I asked what "expecting" meant, both of them stared at me. Aunt Ima said, "Oh, my goodness, I forgot the younguns were in the house. You know that little pitchers have big ears." My Mama told us to just go outside and play. When we got outside, Ida Claire explained to me that "expecting" meant to be pregnant and that meant somebody was going to have a baby. Shoot, I never had thought about all those fancy words. Anyway, we learned our lesson about being around grown-ups when they were talking seriously. Ida Claire explained to me right then that you just have to act like you don't hear a word they're saying to each other. "You just have to keep right on playing."

So we went right into that kitchen and got our water. Ida Claire said to me, "Are you ready to go put on our holsters, Partner? Then we can have a quick-draw!"

I had learned my lesson from before, so I said, "Shoot, yeah, I bet I can draw my gun faster than you!" We went out the back door.

When we got down the steps of the porch, Ida Claire said, "I don't know what Katie and the door have to do with Jesse, but maybe Franklin will know." But, right then, Franklin wasn't anywhere around. And I had on my white pearl-handled guns. So, I started practicing pulling my gun out as fast as I could. This was one thing that I could beat Ida Claire doing. I had to prove that I was "the fastest gun in the West!"

Chapter 5

No Fudging

Three marbles were how many I put in my pocket before I went to Ida Claire's house. I looked out the window and saw that Dewey was at our marble holes in Ida Claire's yard. I decided to go back and get two more of my marbles, just in case Dewey said that we had to play for "Keeps." Sometimes I lost some of my marbles that way. Anyway, I wanted to show Ida Claire the new cat's-eye that Daddy found on Main Street next to the curb. It was an orange cat's-eye marble. And I loved the color orange. Ida Claire said that nobody in her class last year chose orange as their favorite color. But, she said that I was entitled to my own opinion. Sometimes when she told me things like that, I was pretty sure that only one of us knew what she meant. But, that didn't stop us from playing together every chance we got.

Ida Claire stepped out her back door just about the time I stepped up on her porch. She had seen Dewey at the marble holes, too. She had two marbles in her pocket. Her favorite one was a blue-green color. She said it was called turquoise. She said that the other name for it was aquamarine. It looked just plain blue-green to me. We both had a marble that looked like a little white cloud ball with different colors swirled around on it. One of my favorite of those had orange, yellow, and black swirls. Franklin told me that it was called a calico marble. He sure was smart!

When Franklin played, he liked to use a "steelie". It was a shiny, silver marble. He said it was really a ball bearing. All I knew was that if it hit my glass marble just right, it would bust it to pieces.

Ida Claire called out to Dewey, "You having fun?"

Dewey said, "N - N - Naw, not really, j - j - just practicing some." Dewey lived across the back alley right behind Ida

Claire's house. If he wanted to play marbles, he would always come over to play at our marble holes. We really did have a good place. Ida Claire and I had worked a whole day getting the holes just right. First, we cleared off a pretty good size patch. We got all the grass and weeds up and tried to sweep away as many little pebbles as we could. We had it pretty close to the line of cherry laurel trees. That way we had some shade to sit under if it wasn't our turn when a real game was being played. We had three holes in a line and the fourth hole went out like the bottom of a capital letter "L". But the holes were really set up like an upside down "L" that looked almost like a standing-up-straight 7. The day we made the holes Ida Claire measured how far apart they should be by walking off seven footsteps on the dirt between each hole. We worked until we had all four holes the same size. Franklin helped get them nice and deep and smooth with his pocket knife. When we finished, a marble could be shot into the hole and it would stay. We didn't have to worry about it bouncing out. Anyway, our marble holes were the best on the block. And Dewey had come to practice.

We weren't real sure exactly how old Dewey was. We didn't think that he was as old as Franklin, but we knew that he was older than Ida Claire. He always said that he hated to go to school. But I thought he must have liked it pretty good because he had stayed in every grade two times. Ida Claire said that he had flunked every grade. When she said that word "flunked", she made a face like that word tasted bad in her mouth. I really thought he was a little different because he always went barefooted. Of course, we all liked to go barefooted in the summertime, but Dewey didn't like to wear shoes even in the winter when it was freezing. His Mama made him wear them to school. But, he wouldn't wear socks and as soon as he came home, he would kick them off and go outside barefooted. It made Ida Claire and me cold just to look at him. When I asked Mama why he stayed in every grade twice, she just said that it was hard for him to learn. When I asked Franklin why he stayed in every grade twice, Franklin said, "Because he's just plain stupid."

Anyway, he might have been stupid in school things, BUT he could really play a game of marbles. That's why I lost so many marbles because he usually wanted to play for "Keeps." He didn't talk real plain, but we knew when he meant to get one or all of our marbles. We also knew that some of his words were bad words to say. Franklin called it "cussing". Ida Claire and Franklin both knew that if Aunt Ima heard them say a "cussing" word, she would wash their mouths out with soap. Aunt Ima didn't really like for us to play marbles with Dewey. She said that she wouldn't trust him any farther than she could throw a bull by the tail. But, since we were in our own yard, she knew we would probably be safe.

"W - W - We can lag for t - t - taw to see who goes first." We all went to stand at the top of the fourth hole. Ida Claire threw her blue-green marble. It landed about two handspans from taw hole. I threw mine, and it landed a little bit closer to the first hole than Ida Claire's. Then Dewey threw his and it went almost in the hole. He said, "G - G - Good, I go f - f - first." Ida Claire told Dewey that we weren't playing for "Keeps." He told her that would be fine. We didn't have to. He plopped down on his knees, grabbed his marble, made a handspan, and flicked that marble with his thumb. He missed the second hole. It was my turn next since I was next closest when we lagged for taw. I shot and my marble went in. So, I got to try for the third hole. I put my thumb right on the edge of the second hole and shot my marble again. It went right to the side of the next hole. Then it was Ida Claire's turn. She made her handspan. She shot and rang the hole. She might could have tried to shoot Dewey's marble out to no-man's land, but she didn't. She was like me. We knew it was safer not to get Dewey mad about his marble game because he might hit your marble so hard that it would bust it. So Ida Claire just kept playing through. She rang the third hole and shot for the fourth. She missed that one. Dewey took his turn next. He shot towards my marble instead of the next hole. He hit my marble so I had to go back to taw and start over. Then he shot for the next hole and got it. He rang the fourth hole and got Ida Claire's marble in his handspan.

He said, "Tap ties, no any," and shot off of her marble with his. That gave him another shot. But, he missed the next hole. He said, "I ain't sh - sh - shooting too good today." Ida Claire grinned at me. We kept playing just as hard as we could. Dewey really wasn't playing as good as he usually did.

I won that first game! I said, "It must be my lucky orange cat's-eye that made me win."

We began our second game. I kept playing with my lucky marble. Ida Claire kept playing with her favorite blue-green. Dewey changed his blue marble to a red one. "M - M - Maybe I'll get l - l - lucky this time," Dewey said. But, Ida Claire won the second game. Dewey asked if we wanted to play one more game. He told us that he really wasn't having a very good day. Then he pulled out a new marble that we hadn't seen before. He said that maybe this one would bring him some luck. It sure was pretty. It was clear and sparkly all at the same time. Ida Claire's eyes liked to popped out of her head she looked at that marble so hard. Right before we lagged to see who would go first, Dewey asked if we wanted to play for "Keeps" this time. He told us that this wasn't his lucky day, so one of us had a chance to win his brand new marble. Ida Claire and I walked over to the edge of the yard. We were whispering and talking it over. We decided that we had been doing so good that one of us was bound to win!

We started the game, but it didn't last long. As a matter of fact, Dewey went up and down all the marble holes and won the game without Ida Claire and me even getting a turn. He held out his hand. I sure hated to do it, but, shoot, I had to put my orange cat's-eye in his hand. Ida Claire put in her blue-green marble, too. Dewey said, "I had f - f - fun!" Then he headed towards his house. I think that was the first time that he had smiled all day.

Ida Claire looked at me and said, "Now you know why Mama wouldn't trust him any farther that she could throw a bull by the tail." I just looked down at the ground, kicked up some dust, and said, "Yeah." But I wondered when Aunt Ima had played marbles with Dewey!

Chapter 6

Getting Ready, Beads And All

Three Saturdays ago Ida Claire had started saving her allowance for something she found at Roses' dime store. What she wanted cost 29 cents. So it took her three weeks to save enough money. Today was really a special Saturday because Hannah was home for the weekend. She told Ida Claire and me that she would take us to the picture show that afternoon. Hannah said that today the picture show had a double feature. Ida Claire didn't know exactly what that meant. And, shoot, I sure didn't have any idea. We asked Hannah what that meant. She told us, "A double feature means that two different movies will be showing. That means we will get two for the price of one." She seemed to like that, so we did, too. But the thing that Ida Claire liked the most was that we would walk right by the dime store going to the show and coming back from the show. And I had found two things that I really wanted at the dime store, too. I would just have to decide which one to buy today. We figured we could talk Hannah into stopping there one way or another.

The show didn't start until 2:00 that afternoon, and we had just finished breakfast so we had time to play something. We decided we would get our toy cars and trucks. We could drive them around on the dirt in our make-like town. Just on the other side of the marble holes was the perfect spot for the town. It had some grass, but not too much. I got my blue truck and three of my little metal cars. Ida Claire found her green rubber tractor. It used to be Franklin's when he was little, but he gave it to Ida Claire. She said that he told her he wouldn't be playing with that baby thing anymore. She was glad because she always did like that tractor. We got some cigar boxes, a few spools, and we headed to "our town". Ida Claire ran back to her house and asked Aunt Ima for an old round pan that would be alright to get dirty. She came back with an old pie pan. Then we talked about what kind of town we could make today. Two of the cigar boxes were going to be stores. One of the cigar boxes would be a house. Ida Claire said she could use the pie pan at the house. I didn't ask how she would use it. I just waited to see. Ida Claire usually had a pretty good plan about things. Sometimes she would go ahead and tell me what she was planning to do, and sometimes I just had to wait and see. Today was one of the "wait and see" days. We started clearing the roads to the town by pulling up some of the grass that had grown in since the last time we played there. Then we started on the streets. We smoothed and patted the dirt for each street. Some of them would curve and others were straight. Ida Claire asked me if I wanted to put the house on one of the curves. I said, "Shoot, Ida Claire, I reckon that's as good a place as any." I just wanted to see what she was going to do with that pie pan. So we set the cigar box at one of the curves. Ida Claire told me to go get some twigs off the cherry laurel tree and she went to get some little limbs from the mimosa. She stood the twigs in the ground and put some of the fern-leaves from the mimosa beside them.

"Now, we have the shrubbery for the house," she said. Then she went and got a stick. She started digging out a hole a little bit bigger around than the pie pan. She made it look just about as deep as the pie pan, too. Then I saw what the pie pan could be. She placed it right in the hole she had just dug and then patted the dirt back around the pan. She told me to go get some water. I knew then that our house in our town would soon have a backyard swimming pool. While I went to get the water, Ida Claire stood the spools on one end close to the pan. "How do you like the tables by the pool, Will?"

"I like them just fine. I wish we really did have a big swimming pool in the backyard," I said. Ida Claire told me that I was wishing that because I would rather get in the pool than go take a bath.

Ida Claire said, "When Hannah sees those dirt beads around your neck and under your arms, she is going to make you go get a bath for sure." Ida Claire liked to tease me about my beads. But, shoot, we always played hard and I didn't want to wear a hot shirt in the summertime. I remember one time Ida Claire told me that boys sure were lucky because they didn't have to wear shirts. Ida Claire said that we didn't have much time left to play because it was almost time for dinner. I thought my stomach was feeling empty for something.

Hannah walked over to where we were playing. She looked and said, "What a nice swimming pool behind your house here at the curve!" I looked at Ida Claire and grinned. Hannah was someone that could appreciate what we did when we played. She was really nice that way. She usually did some really good things with us when she was home. And today the really good thing was going to be taking us to the picture show. "Will, you and Ida Claire need to go wash your hands because it's time for lunch. And, Will, wipe those beads off from your neck and under your arms."

Then, Ida Claire looked at me and grinned. She said, "Hannah, if Will washes his beads off now, he won't need to take a bath, will he?"

Hannah said, "Oh, no, he will definitely still need a bath!" I gave Ida Claire a "thank you for trying" look and all three of us walked to the house.

Ida Claire stuck her head in her back door to ask Aunt Ima if she could eat at my house. Aunt Ima said that the whole family was going to eat there. I had forgotten that when Hannah was home sometimes Mama cooked for both families to eat together. We had roast beef and gravy, rice, peas, pear salad, and big biscuits. Aunt Ima brought in her yummy corn and a peach cobbler. Hannah said, "This meal is fit for a king." I didn't know about a king, but I knew it was fit for a hungry little boy that had just wiped the dirt beads off his neck a few minutes ago.

After we finished eating Hannah said, "Okay, Will, you'll have just enough time to go get a good bath and we'll be ready to walk to the show." I wrinkled my nose, but I knew there was no need to fuss about it.

Aunt Ima's next sentence made me feel a lot better about it though. "And, Ida Claire, you need to go get a bath, too, because I've gotten something new that you can wear today." Ida Claire jumped right up and didn't seem to be bothered by a bath as much as I was. But, maybe, the new outfit made the difference for her.

Chapter 7

Getting Our Money's Worth

Three folks just walking hand in hand on the sidewalk. That's how we looked as we started to town. Hannah walked in the middle. And I could tell by the way that Ida Claire walked that she really liked her new outfit. She had on black pedal-pushers. These were like long shorts that came to her knees. When I wore long shorts that came to my knees, they were called Calypso pants. I just didn't understand why grown-ups couldn't call them one name for everybody. Sometimes grown-ups just didn't make sense to me. Ida Claire had on a purple and black shirt and some flip-flops. She really liked her new outfit. Hannah told her that she looked real pretty. And Ida Claire grinned from ear to ear. She said, "I asked Mama if she thought I looked pretty and she said, 'Pretty is as pretty does'." Then she said that sometimes Aunt Ima answers her with "Beauty is only skin deep." When Ida Claire talked like that, was the only time I thought of her as being a girl. She really was more of a tomboy. She didn't even care if anybody called her a tomboy. All I knew was that she played really fun stuff better than a lot of boys and I liked playing with her better than anybody else.

We walked past the Rotary clubhouse, and I told Hannah about the day that Ida Claire hurt her elbow. And I told her about the neat sling. Ida Claire showed her the scar. Hannah said that she wouldn't have liked seeing all that blood, so she was glad she wasn't home when it happened. Ida Claire said, "Hannah, Mama didn't even whip me."

And I said, "Yeah, wonders never cease!"

While we were telling the story, we went past Mrs. Lockett's house on the corner and then past the Ford place. That's where Uncle Ben worked, but we didn't see him when we looked in the windows. We turned the corner and went by the restaurant and furniture store. Next were the two dime stores. One was Roses' and the other was Ben Franklin's 5 & 10. Ida Claire reached her hand in her pocket and jiggled her three dimes. I looked up at Hannah. She said, "We'll stop by here on our way back home. We don't want to be late or we'll miss the cartoons and the previews of coming attractions." Then, I looked at Ida Claire and we both shrugged our shoulders. We kept walking and went past Belks, the bank, another drugstore, and a department store. We turned the corner and could see the Martin Theater sign. It was in the next block. We went past the doctor's office. There was a sign hanging out from the doorway that said, "Dr. Phil A. Kneed, M.D.". Hannah said that it certainly was appropriate for a doctor to have that name, and then she laughed. She was using those fancy words again. Shoot, I didn't know what she thought was so funny either. Every time I went to Dr. Kneed's office I had to have a shot to get ready to start school. I sure hoped that school didn't hurt as much as those shots did! We crossed the street and went past Mr. Barlow's barber shop. I waved at Mr. Barlow, and he threw up one of his hands and waved back. We didn't have to wait in line at the ticket window. We were glad. Aunt Ima had given Hannah a quarter to pay for Ida Claire to go to the show. And Hannah gave me a quarter, too. She told us to pay our own way and gave Ida Claire her quarter. The lady behind the glass window with a hole in it gave us back some money. Ida Claire said that we each had a dime to spend for some candy or popcorn. We stepped through the door and gave the tickets to the man. He tore them in half and gave one side back to us. The good smell of popcorn was all in the lobby. Hannah said that we could choose what we wanted to buy with our money. I picked popcorn. I thought I got a pretty good deal to get such a big bag of popcorn for such a little piece of money. Ida Claire bought red hots candy with her dime. And then we both would get to eat popcorn and red hots because we would share.

We walked on in to find our seats. We were just in time because it was starting to get dark. We found a good place about in the middle of all the seats. Hannah sat between us because we both wanted to sit beside her. Then, it started getting darker and darker. It was so dark that I kept blinking. I couldn't tell if my eyes were opened or closed. Then, the sound started and the light started showing up front. We saw pictures about shows we didn't really know about. Hannah told us that those were previews of coming attractions. She acted like she knew what she was talking about. I sure didn't. But we were at the picture show and the popcorn was good. The cartoons came on next. It was "Mickey Mouse", and Ida Claire and I both loved to watch cartoons. Sometimes we would watch them early on Saturday morning. In this cartoon Mickey was whistling and trying to get Minnie to dance with him. Everybody in the show was laughing.

The cartoon was over and Hannah told us that it was time for the first show in our double feature. The music started and it sounded a little bit scary to me. It showed a big house at night. Then we saw a man wearing a white coat. Hannah said that he was a doctor in his laboratory. The doctor in the show started talking and used big words that I didn't really understand. I heard the word "vampire". Then the music got really scary. I started hiding my eyes and didn't watch too much of it. When I looked at Ida Claire, she had her hands over her face. She would open her fingers a little and peek between them. It sure was dark in the picture show. Hannah said that she didn't know that the show was going to be like this today. She asked us if we were ready to leave, and if we were getting scared. Ida Claire said, "No, we hadn't gotten our money's worth." And, shoot, I didn't want to be a sissy about it. So, I said that we could stay, too. Most of the time I didn't watch, but I did see that doctor man come from the graveyard and I saw him grab a woman and leave two holes in her neck. When Hannah saw THAT, she said that we just had to leave. I didn't know how Ida Claire and Hannah felt, but I was mighty glad that she decided to leave.

We stepped out of the show and the bright sun made our eyes feel like they would pop out of our heads. But, I was glad to get out of that graveyard. Ida Claire asked Hannah, "Why was that doctor a vampire? And why did he get the blood from that woman's neck?" I didn't know how Ida Claire saw all of that when she was just peeking through her fingers. Hannah told her that there is really no such thing as a vampire and there is nothing to be scared about really. And as long as the sun was shining, I almost believed her.

I heard Ida Claire jiggle the dimes in her pocket again. I was glad we were going to the dime store. I knew since it was daylight, there wouldn't be any vampires in there. We went straight to the toy section first. Ida Claire knew exactly what she wanted. So, she said that she would help me choose what I wanted. "Did you say a slingshot might be one of the things you wanted, Will?" Ida Claire asked me. I told her that Franklin called it a flip instead.

I told her, "I can't decide between a flip and a cap-gun that shoots caps." Hannah said that I could get one of those this time and maybe get the other one next time. I decided to get the flip. Then Hannah asked Ida Claire what she wanted.

Ida Claire said, "Y'all just follow me and you'll see the prettiest thing in the store." We went to the jewelry case. Ida Claire showed us a ring that had a dark green stone in it. The price tag was 29 cents. She told me that the tax would be a penny. So she had just enough money. The lady took the ring out of the case and let Ida Claire try it on. It was perfect. We paid for our things and went out of the store grinning. Ida Claire held out her hand with the ring on it. Hannah told her that it was so pretty it looked like a little green crown sitting on her finger. Ida Claire said that it felt so good that it felt like it was made for her hand. I squeezed my flip in my hand. Shoot, it felt just right, too. And I decided it was made for my hand. I couldn't wait to get home to try it out.

Chapter 8

Ain't No Booger Men Out Tonight

"Three different families are coming to the house tonight, Will!" Ida Claire told me the next Saturday. I said, "Really, why?" She explained to me that Aunt Ima and Uncle Ben had invited all those folks for a fish fry. "You know all of them, Will. And the best part is that it'll be a heap of kids here!" I told her that that sounded all right to me. Then I asked her, "What boys are coming?" I really didn't care if any girls came or not, except, of course, Ida Claire. But, she didn't really count as a girl.

Ida Claire told me that the Hixons would be coming. I wrinkled my nose because I didn't know who the Hixons were. Ida Claire said, "You do know them, too, Will!" They live out in the country and we went to their house the first week I got out of school for the summer. My Mama and your Mama wanted to go pick some butterbeans from their garden. While our Mamas picked the beans we played with Harry, Timmy, and Patsy." After Ida Claire told me all of that I did remember who she was talking about. They were pretty fun to play with. Ida Claire reminded me about the snake that Aunt Ima saw.

"Oh, yeah," I said. "When Aunt Ima saw that snake, she threw that sack of beans up in the air and took off running towards the car." I got tickled just thinking about it. Ida Claire laughed, too.

Then she said, "Yeah, and Miss Belle told her that it was just a king snake and wouldn't hurt her, BUT, Mama said that it would make her hurt herself!" I sure didn't know that Aunt Ima could run so fast. Yeah, I liked the Hixon kids. I was glad they were coming to the fish fry that night.

The McGee family was supposed to come, too! Mr. Bud and Miss Ruth always played cards with Aunt Ima and Uncle Ben.

They loved to play set-back. Sometimes Ida Claire and I would get to deal the cards for them if we didn't talk and giggle too much. I asked Ida Claire if Hannah was going to teach us that set-back card game. Ida Claire said that it must have been just for grown ups and was probably a lot harder than canasta. Shoot, canasta was plenty hard enough for me right now. I sure didn't want anything any harder! Ida Claire usually grinned a lot when Mr. Bud was at their house. He always teased her about the rings on her fingers. He knew how much she loved to wear them. Tonight I bet she would be sure to show him that new green ring she bought. There were two McGee kids, Sarah and Billy. Billy like to play all of our nighttime games. And Sarah was close to Franklin's age. She was so busy watching to see what Franklin was doing that she didn't really bother me.

The other family that would be there was our Uncle Jim, Aunt JoEllen, and their boy, Jimmy. Jimmy was my age. We usually played pretty good together. Or, at least, I could say we played pretty good together about the first thirty minutes. Then, I don't know why, but for some reason we always started tussling. And then, he would get mad, and I would get mad, and we would just turn our tussling into a straight fight. That's why if Aunt JoEllen ever let me come play with Jimmy, she'd always ask Ida Claire, too. She said that Ida Claire had to be our referee. Anyway, as long as other kids were around, we usually played pretty good together.

It was still daylight when the other families started coming to Ida Claire's. Franklin, Ida Claire, and I were setting up the volleyball net. Counting the three of us there would be nine children in all. Uncle Jim might play with us, too. That way the sides would be even. Uncle Ben had the fish cooker heating up in the backyard. And Aunt Ima and Mama were in the kitchen getting the slaw, French fries, and hushpuppies ready. As soon as all the kids got there, we started our volleyball game. Shoot, I tried the best I could, but, I think I needed to be a little taller to get that ball over the net. It seemed like every point went to the team that had the tallest players to hit it. But, we still had fun.

Ida Claire and I had gotten thirsty and we walked around to the back porch to go inside and get a drink of water. Uncle Jim asked us if we wanted to see how to strike a match without touching it. We said, "Yes, Sir!" The fish cooker was almost full of hot oil. He took a match and laid it in the oil. All of a sudden the match lit. Uncle Jim said, "Okay, it's hot enough to put the fish in now." Aunt Ima brought the fish out to Uncle Ben in a brown paper grocery sack. Uncle Ben would shake the sack, then take out a fish that was covered in meal. Then, he would put that fish in the fish cooker. It started smelling good as soon as that first fish went into the grease. We finished our water and then went back to the front yard where the other kids were. Franklin and Sarah were taking down the volleyball net. Franklin told us that when we started playing after supper, it would be dark and we didn't need anybody running into the net if we played "tag".

Harry asked if anybody wanted to play "Sling the Statue". All of us said that we did. Since Harry thought of the game, he got to be the first "slinger". He started with Franklin. He grabbed Franklin's hands and they went around and around. Then, Harry slung Franklin off. Franklin kept spinning and turning around until Harry said, "Freeze!". Then, we would each take a turn trying to guess what "statue" Franklin was being. Timmy guessed that Franklin was a football player. That was right. So then, Franklin grabbed Timmy and "slung" him around and around. When Timmy froze, Patsy guessed that he was turning somersaults. He shook his head. I guessed that he was a ball rolling. He shook his head again. Everybody guessed but nobody guessed it right. He finally told us that he was a tumbleweed in the wind out on a desert. About that time Aunt Ima called for us to come wash our hands and get ready for supper. Ida Claire whispered to me on the way to the sink, "That Timmy has a good imagination. We need to remember that tumbleweed statue the next time we play."

Uncle Ben was spooning in the hushpuppies when we started getting in line to get our plates. Aunt JoEllen asked us if we knew why they were called hushpuppies. We told her that we didn't. She said that a long time ago when someone was trying to cook some bread outside over an open fire, that a dog kept barking. And that person threw some of that bread at the dog so he would eat it and quit barking. Then, the man told the dog, "Now, Hush, Puppy!" Franklin sorta whispered to Ida Claire and me, "It would be pretty funny if we called them 'Shut-up, Dogs' instead of hushpuppies!" Uncle Ben told everybody to bow their heads and he would say the blessing. But Ida Claire and I didn't hear a word of the blessing because we were trying not to be too loud when we were laughing just thinking about what Franklin had said.

As soon as Mr. Bud saw Ida Claire, he noticed her ring. He said, "Let me see that pretty ring." She showed it to him and grinned a big grin.

When we started through the line, Aunt Ima told everybody to be sure and get two of those paper plates. Since the plates were flimsy she knew that the food might dump out on the ground. Uncle Ben told everybody, "Y'all help yourself, there's a gracious plenty for everybody!" All of us went through the line putting fish, French fries, and hushpuppies on our plates. Ida Claire shook the ketchup bottle and poured some on her plate and mine. Ida Claire, Jimmy, Patsy, Timmy, and I took our plates to our Mamas. One really good thing about still being little was that a grown-up would pick out our fish for us. So, we just had the good meaty part. We didn't have to worry about getting choked or swallowing a bone. I didn't know how old you had to be to not get your fish picked out, but I knew Franklin was past the time. And tonight I was glad that I was still little because I was just about to starve, and I sure didn't want to worry about any little fish bones going down my throat.

By the time we finished eating, it had gotten dark. All the grown-ups got folding outside chairs and sat around the table talking. That meant we had time to go around to the front of the house and play some more games. The corner streetlight was the only light we had. It caused us to make shadows while we were playing. Franklin asked if we wanted to play "Hide-and-Seek". Shoot, we all liked that game. Franklin said that he would be "It" and would hide his eyes first. He started counting to one hundred.

Before we ran to hide, we skipped around him singing, "Ain't no booger men out tonight ... Grandpa killed them all last night!" Then, we ran to hide.

After Franklin counted to one hundred he said, "Ready or not, here I come!" Two kids went to hide in the mimosa tree. Three went to different places in the ditch. Jimmy ran to the corner of the house. But, Ida Claire and I went to hide on the ground by the corner of the front porch. We squatted down behind the nandina bushes. The shadows must have hidden us pretty good. Franklin found all the other kids. But, Ida Claire and I just kept squatting and kept quiet. I really don't think Franklin would have found us except that Aunt JoEllen said that it was time for Jimmy to go home. Then, all the other grown-ups said that they needed to call it a night, too. Aunt Ima said for Ida Claire to come show her manners. So, we climbed out and Ida Claire said, "We enjoyed having y'all to come play with us!" They all said that they enjoyed it, too! I liked all of it, too. Except, now they knew where the best hiding place was for our "Hide-and-Seek" game. Shoot, we really did fool them one time anyway.

Chapter 9

Country Climbing

Three days after the fish fry Aunt JoEllen and Jimmy came to the house. They wanted to know if I wanted to go with them out to the country to visit Aunt Frances and her family. She was really only Jimmy's aunt and not mine, but that's what I called her anyway. Mama was planning on going, too. Aunt JoEllen said, "Of course, Ida Claire needs to go to be the referee when you two boys get in a fight." Jimmy and I ran over to Ida Claire's house to see if Aunt Ima would let her go. Aunt Ima said that that would be fine. The three kids piled in the back seat of Aunt JoEllen's black car. Ida Claire sat in the middle. Ida Claire asked me if I remembered Phillip and Cynthia. I told her I did. They were Aunt Frances's children. Cynthia was a year older than Ida Claire and Phillip was a year older than Jimmy and me.

Then Ida Claire said, "Will, you weren't able to come the last time we went to Aunt Frances's house. We really had a great time though. There will be all sorts of adventures for us today!" Ida Claire called her Aunt Frances, too, but she wasn't really kin to Ida Claire either.

I asked Ida Claire what sort of adventures was she talking about. She said just to wait and see. Mama told us to play a game while we were riding because we still had a little while to go. Jimmy said, "Let's play 'I Spy'. I'll start." Ida Claire said that we needed to have some rules before we started. She said that we need to make sure everybody can see whatever we spy and that it's something inside the car. I asked her why she thought we needed rules. She told me that it would keep Jimmy and me from fussing. I said, "Oh."

Aunt JoEllen said, "That's good."

In no time at all we were turning onto the dirt road to get to Phillip's house. It seemed like Aunt JoEllen was driving mighty slow. Jimmy finally asked, "What's taking so long?" She told him it was because of the bumps and ruts in the road. Then as we got closer to the house, she went even slower because of all the dogs. Any day you went to Aunt Frances's house you could see at least ten to fifteen dogs. Ida Claire started counting. She counted thirteen little dogs. She always said that was one thing that she didn't like about going there. She didn't like dogs. As a matter of fact, she was scared of dogs if they were very big. Before, when I had asked her why she was scared of dogs, she said it was because they could bite you. But I knew a dog had never bitten her. But Franklin always said that it was because Aunt Ima told Ida Claire that the old black dog got her bottle when she was little. I reckon I wouldn't like dogs too much either if one had taken my bottle when I was a baby. When we got out of the car, I called the dogs over to me. Then Ida Claire could get out and not be too scared. These were little dogs so she was all right with them. At least, she tried to act like she wasn't scared.

Phillip came running out of the house. He had some ropes in his hands. He said, "I thought y'all would never get here. Mama said that we could go to the red clay banks down by the sandpits." Shoot, that sounded like a good idea to me. Ida Claire, Jimmy, and I grinned at each other. But, Aunt JoEllen and Mama raised their eyebrows like they wanted to tell us no.

They looked at Aunt Frances. She said, "Oh, the younguns will be okay. Phillip and Cynthia play there all the time." So we took off running before our Mamas changed their minds.

Mama yelled, "Y'all be careful and watch out for snakes."

I knew a good adventure was about to begin. First, Phillip showed us the last place on the side of the bank that he had practiced his "mountain-climbing". Then Cynthia showed us the place where she had climbed the last time. Ida Claire, Jimmy, and I looked at each other. I didn't know what they were thinking, but that clay bank looked more like a real mountain to me. It was mighty high and it went almost straight up. It was about as tall as all our daddies if they stood on each other's shoulders. I sure hoped I could climb it and not fall. I had to try because I didn't want to be called a "chicken". When I looked back at Ida Claire, she looked like she was thinking the same thing. But, then she whispered to me, "Will, we'll do like the little engine that said, 'I think I can'."

Phillip had started his climb. He had the ropes up on his shoulder around one arm. He was climbing up that bank almost like it had stairs in the dirt. Cynthia laughed and said that she thought he must be part mountain goat. We all laughed then. When Phillip got to the top, he took one of the ropes and tied it to a tree. Then, he threw that rope back over the edge and it dangled down just right for the next person to climb.

He laughed and said, "Look at my snake. I'm throwing it over the mountain." Ida Claire, Jimmy, and I decided we would wait a little bit longer before we climbed. Cynthia hollered up to Phillip to tie another rope on the tree that was at the top of where she usually climbed. It wasn't quite as straight up there. Since Cynthia was the oldest, she said that she would wait until we climbed up first. She said that she would be at the bottom to catch us if we slipped and fell. I sure didn't want to find out if she would really be able to catch me or not. Jimmy went up the rope next. Ida Claire and I couldn't decide who should try the climb next. Cynthia started with "Eeny, meeny, miney, moe" to decide for us. I got the last "moe", so I was next. I grabbed the rope and held on tight. It seemed like that bank was as tall as the tallest tree I had ever seen. But, I finally made it. From the top I yelled down to Ida Claire, "Come on up, you can do it." So, Ida Claire did climb right up to where I was. Then, Cynthia came up.

We played up on top for a little while. Then Cynthia said that we better get back because our Mamas might be a little worried. She climbed down first. Ida Claire climbed down next. I grabbed the rope and started backing down slowly. Jimmy said that he wasn't ready to go yet. All of a sudden, Phillip looked sorta white and he almost shouted, "We've got to get down from here right now!" I guess Jimmy knew that Phillip meant business. They each came down a different rope in a hurry. When they were almost to the ground, Cynthia asked Phillip why he was being so bossy. He told her that a big rattlesnake was at the tree where one of the ropes was tied. That was enough reason for all of us to take off running. When we had gotten almost to the house, Phillip said, "Now, y'all don't say anything about the snake because Mama might not let us play there anymore." We promised we wouldn't say a word. We even "crossed our hearts and hoped to die" if we did tell.

Aunt Frances asked Phillip what he did with his ropes. He told her that he decided to just let them say there until next time. That sounded pretty good to us. But, Ida Claire whispered to me, "Those ropes might rot before the next time I go there."

I told her, "Shoot, I know that's right!"

Chapter 10

Summer Celebration Day

Three cane fishing poles were in the car hooks on top of Daddy's car. When I got out of bed, I saw Daddy getting his fishing tackle together. And since he had more than one pole, that meant that somebody else was going to get to go fishing with him. Today wasn't Saturday or Sunday. I didn't know why Daddy hadn't gone to work yet. So, I asked him. He said, "Today is a holiday, Will. It's July 4th and we're going to celebrate it with your Aunt Ima's family." Whoopee! That sounded like pretty good fun to me.

"And we're going fishing?" I asked.

Daddy said, "Yep! Go see if your Mama is getting the food together." So I went to the kitchen. Sure enough, Mama had a big cardboard box that had sandwiches and chips and a red and white checkered tablecloth in it. I asked Mama if I could go find out what Ida Claire and Franklin were going to take. She said for me to first go look in the drawer and get out my swimsuit. After I found my swimsuit, I hurried over to Ida Claire's house. I had gotten so excited by the time I got to Ida Claire's house that I was jumping up and down.

"Ida Claire, we're going to go fishing and swimming!" I almost shouted.

Ida Claire said, "I know it, Will, and we're going to have a picnic, too." We both started squealing and clapping then.

Uncle Ben told us, "Y'all take all that racket outside. There's no need for all that noise in the house."

We both said, "Yes, sir." Then we ran outside.

"What are you going to take?" I asked Ida Claire. She said that she had to get her swimsuit and her sunglasses. I told her that I wanted to take my float ring since we would be swimming. Then

Franklin came out of the house and he already had on his swimsuit and he was toting a rope. "What do you need a rope for, Franklin?" I asked him.

He told me, "Well, Squirt, maybe, just maybe, we'll get lucky!" I looked at Ida Claire and I could tell that she didn't know what he was talking about either. We went back inside and Ida Claire started looking for her rubber ball that we could use to play kickball. She got a deck of cards, too. Mama came over to talk with Aunt Ima to see if she needed to bring anything else. Aunt Ima told her that she had made the potato salad, fried chicken, and brownies. She was looking around the kitchen for something. Mama asked her what she needed. Aunt Ima told her that she wanted the thermos to put in some iced tea. She asked Mama to go look in the pantry. She was looking. Then, Aunt Ima walked in and moved over a few cans.

She finally spotted it and said, "I can't see for looking." She called for Franklin to get the ice chest and get the ice out of the ice trays to put in there. That was for the cokes. Uncle Ben said that he was going over to check to see what tackle Hiram had packed. "Okey, dokey, we're just about ready in here," Aunt Ima said. She called for Ida Claire to get three quilts we could spread for the picnic.

We finally were ready to load the car. With all the ice chests, cardboard boxes, and the fishing tackle the trunks of both cars were just about full. Mama said, "We need to get the folding outside chairs." Aunt Ima sent Franklin to get theirs and Ida Claire and I went to get ours. When it was time to get in the cars, Ida Claire asked if I wanted to ride with them. I asked Mama if I could and she said that that would be fine.

Right then, Franklin and Ida Claire both called, "Shotgun." I wanted to be able to sit by the window, too. Oh, well, maybe next time I could be the first to say it.

After we had gotten out of the city limits, Franklin asked, "Daddy, where are we going fishing exactly?" Uncle Ben told him that we were going to Bear Bridge on the Finchakoonee Creek. Ida Claire and I had never been there. We looked at each other and grinned. That sounded like a funny name for a creek. I looked around to see if Mama and Daddy were following us. They weren't back there. I asked Uncle Ben where they were. He told me that they were going to get some bait. He said that Hiram wanted some crickets and worms. Uncle Ben pulled off the paved road and started down a hill that was a dirt road. He stopped the car in a shady spot right before we got to the bridge.

Aunt Ima said, "I think that this will do just fine." All of us started taking the stuff out of the car. When we had cleaned it out, Mama and Daddy drove down the hill.

Franklin, Ida Claire, and I wanted to go swimming first. We walked to the edge of the creek. There was a little bit of sand and a whole lot of little rocks. But, we had been barefooted so much that the bottoms of our feet were tough. Franklin pointed to a tree limb that was hanging out over the water. "Yes, sir, this is my lucky day!" Then, he pulled the rope off of his arm. He asked Uncle Ben if it would be okay to tie a slip knot with his rope onto the limb so we could use it to swing out into the creek. Uncle Ben told him that he would need to check the water he would be jumping into and see how deep it was. He told him to swim down to the bottom and check for big rocks, too. Because, if it was too shallow, none of us needed to be jumping in with a rope or anything else.

We were glad we already had on our swimsuits. Franklin was a good swimmer. He waded into the water and got where he knew the rope would swing. Then, he dove under the water. He stayed underwater for a long time. He came up for air and then went under again. He came back up with a splash. He said, "Everything looks great. There's not even any dead stumps or limbs in this spot." So, he got out and climbed the tree with his rope. He tied a slip knot and shimmied down the rope and dropped in the water. He tied a swinging knot in the bottom of the rope and pulled the rope over to a place he could grab it and swing out. Ida Claire said that he would have to make sure it worked before she would try it. That sounded like a good idea to me, too.

While we waited for Franklin to try out the rope swing, we

waded into the water. It had already gotten hot, so the water felt nice and cool. When we walked slow, the mud came up between our toes. Ida Claire asked me, "Will, do you feel that mud squoosh up between your toes?"

I told her, "Shoot, I sure do. It feels kinda gooshy."

Ida Claire asked Aunt Ima and Mama if they wanted to wade in the water so that they could feel the mud. Aunt Ima said, "Mercy, no! I felt enough chicken stuff between my toes when I was a little girl feeding the chickens in their pen." We laughed. Franklin hollered like an Indian, swung out on his rope, and splashed down in the creek. Aunt Ima said, "He wouldn't give a gold guinea to be doing that!" Daddy and Uncle Ben moved on the other side of the bridge so he wouldn't mess up their fishing. We splashed and swam around some more.

Mama and Aunt Ima said that the picnic was ready. We each climbed out of the creek and wrapped a warm towel around us. Ida Claire's pink swimsuit didn't look so pink anymore. Aunt Ima said, "I'm glad you wore that old swimsuit because creek water turns everything brown." We ate our good lunch. Everything sure does taste extra good after you've been swimming. We had a brownie for dessert. Um - Hum. It was sure enough good. Ida Claire jumped up ready to go back swimming. Aunt Ima said, "Y'all will have to wait for your dinner to settle. You don't need stomach cramps." Franklin said that he saw Raymond bend over double with stomach cramps at the pool one day. That sounded like a good enough reason to me to just sit on the quilt and play cards for a little while. Ida Claire dealt the cards and we played Crazy Eights. I heard Aunt Ima yawn and then she said, "I could stretch a mile if I didn't have to walk back." That was one of her sayings that almost made sense to me.

Franklin went fishing with Uncle Ben and Daddy. He took his favorite spinning rod and reel. In a little while we heard his reel spinning and looked up. The rod was bent way down. He must have gotten a mighty big bream. Sure enough, he pulled it in and it was the size of my Daddy's hand. That was big because my Daddy was a big man. He added it to the stringer that Uncle

Ben was holding. Ida Claire looked at me and said, "Look's like we'll get to have another fish fry soon." The next thing we knew, Daddy and Uncle Ben were showing us two full strings of fish they had caught. Uncle Ben told Franklin to climb up the tree and untie his rope. He said that we would need to get home so that they could get all those fish cleaned.

Franklin said that he wished that Ida Claire and I had had a chance to swing out on his rope. I was kinda glad that I didn't get the chance. It looked pretty scary to me. I probably could have grabbed hold to the rope good enough, but I wasn't too sure about hanging on to that rope long enough to get to the right spot to drop in the water. And, anyway, I was just learning how to swim. Ida Claire must have read my mind. She leaned over and whispered, "I think THAT can wait until we get as old as Franklin." I nodded!

Aunt Ima sighed and said that we had a nice July 4th celebration. She said that everybody seemed to enjoy it. Uncle Ben winked and said, "But, it's not over yet. We've just had our daytime celebration. Later, we'll get to our nighttime celebration." I looked at Ida Claire and Franklin. They both shrugged their shoulders. The best that I could tell, nobody knew what Uncle Ben meant. But, I was getting excited just wondering what else we could do to celebrate.

Chapter 11

Celebration Night

Three big bream and eighteen medium-sized bream had to be cleaned as soon as we got home. Uncle Ben told Franklin, "If you're big enough to catch 'em, you're big enough to clean 'em."

Whew, I was glad that I didn't catch any that day. I went in the house with Ida Claire. Aunt Ima told her that she needed to get in the shower to wash all that dirty creek water out of her hair.

"I'm glad that I have a crewcut. I can get the water hose outside and get that creek water out of mine," I told Ida Claire.

"That's a good idea, Will! Since we both have on our swimsuits, we can play in the sprinkler. I'll have to see if Mama will let me," Ida Claire said. I went to turn on the sprinkler and Ida Claire went to get the shampoo. We ran and splashed and jumped and yelled.

Daddy, Uncle Ben, and Franklin were busy cleaning fish. They had out their pocket knives. Each one had a fish scraping the scales off of it. Those scales were popping off left and right. They looked pretty yucky to me. Ida Claire said, "Pe - ew - ew, they sure do stink!"

Franklin said, "They may stink now, but they'll smell mighty good when you get to eat them!" Ida Claire and I both nodded to that.

Uncle Ben told us to get through at the sprinkler because we would need to get our clothes on so we could continue our celebration. Ida Claire asked him, "What are we going to do next?"

He said, "Well, we just might have to go to your Uncle Buford's and Aunt Bertha's out in the country. We need to see if any kind of celebrating is going on out there!"

"Can Will go, too, Daddy?" Ida Claire asked. He said that that would be okay with him, but it depended what his daddy thought about it. We both looked at Daddy. Ida Claire asked, "Please, Uncle Hiram, can Will go?"

He said, "Well, Curly Top, (that's what he called Ida Claire) I reckon that'll be okay."

"Yippee!" we shouted, grabbed hands, and started jumping up and down and all around going in a circle. It was soon time for us to go to Ida Claire's Aunt Bertha's and Uncle Buford's house. Aunt Bertha was Uncle Ben's sister. So, she wasn't really kin to me, but I called her Aunt Bertha anyway. She and Uncle Buford lived out in the country. I had been riding out there just one other time. It was one Sunday afternoon when I went with Ida Claire.

Uncle Ben came out of the house with a brown paper sack that was full of something. But, he had it rolled down on top and we couldn't tell what was in it. Ida Claire asked, "What do you have in the bag, Daddy?"

Uncle Ben told her, "Oh, this will make us have a big July 4th celebration!" I looked at Ida Claire. She didn't know what was in the sack either.

When I looked at Franklin, he grinned and said, "You just wait, Squirt. You really will be jumping up and down when you see that!"

It was time to get in the car. Ida Claire whispered to me, "Say 'shotgun' with me, Will, right now!" While she was saying it, Franklin shouted it and I did, too. Ida Claire said, "Oh, well, I'll sit in the middle." I didn't tell Ida Claire "thank you" but I looked at her with my "I'm-glad-you-helped-me" look! So Franklin sat by one back seat window and I sat by the other.

Finally, we got to Uncle Buford's. It was still daylight. Grown-ups called this time of day "dusk!" Uncle Ben said, "It will be windy tomorrow!" Ida Claire asked him how he knew. He said, "If the sun sets red, it will be windy the next day."

Uncle Buford told us to come look at his prize sow. While we were walking around to the back, Ida Claire asked me if I had ever heard her Mama tell the "pig story". I sure hadn't heard Aunt Ima tell about that. Ida Claire asked her Mama to please tell me the story.

Aunt Ima said, "Well, it's not much of a story really. But, I'll tell you the part Ida Claire is talking about. When I was a little girl, one of my chores was to 'slop the hogs'. That means that I had to feed the pigs. So, I would take the mush to the pigpen and pour it in their trough. On the way to the trough, sometimes, the sow would get in my way. Then I would yell, 'Su - ey, suey'. And that would make the pig move out of the way. Then, I would call, 'Pig, pig, pig-o'. And those little short-legged pigs would come running!" Aunt Ima's voice made a high squeaky sound when she was talking to the pigs. Ida Claire and I just giggled and giggled. Aunt Ima sure made a good pig-caller. We had gotten to the pigpen by the time that Aunt Ima finished her story.

Ida Claire, Franklin, and I climbed up on the wooden slats on the front side of the pen. Whew! That was the biggest pig I had ever seen. Uncle Buford said, "She looks mean and fierce, don't she? But, Ol' Susie is just as gentle as a lamb. It will be okay if the little ones want to ride her back."

Now, that really did sound like fun to me. Uncle Buford asked us which one wanted to go first. I looked at Ida Claire and she pointed to me. I told Uncle Buford that I would. He climbed into the pigpen and reached up to pull me over the wooden fence. He put me on top of Ol' Susie's back. She was so fat that my legs almost stuck straight out. The only problem was that I didn't really have anything to hold on to. But, Uncle Buford was walking beside me. He turned Ol' Susie so she wouldn't head toward the big mud puddle at the other end of the pen. Then, he walked us back to Ida Claire. He asked Ida Claire if she wanted to ride, too. Ida Claire said she would if she could get behind me. Uncle Buford said, "Well, I don't reckon there will be any harm in that." So, he grabbed Ida Claire and put her right behind me. Her legs stuck out, too. And Ol' Susie started walking again. Ida Claire and I got to laughing.

Aunt Ima said, "Now, that's a sight for sore eyes!"

Now, I don't know if Ol' Susie had gotten her feelings hurt or if she decided that Ida Claire and me were just too heavy. But, all of a sudden, she took off running to the mud hole. And we were trying to hold on, but that was hard to do. Uncle Buford was running along side saying, "Whoa, Susie, whoa!" And Susie finally did stop. Just as soon as she got to the mud hole, she stopped dead still. But Ida Claire and I didn't. We went flying over Ol' Susie's head and went plop right in the mud. We both looked at each other and started laughing. We weren't hurt.

Then Franklin walked over and said, "Squirts, we're company that's visiting, and now is not the time to make mud pies." Then, he bent over double and his face turned red he was laughing so hard.

Aunt Ima told us to climb out and she would wash us off under the water hose. Two times in one day under the hose was a pretty good way to spend July 4th, I thought. She said that it was hot enough that our clothes would dry soon anyway. Uncle Buford started an outdoor fire while we were being washed. Then, Aunt Bertha brought out some hot dogs and coat hangers. That was a mighty good surprise. She said, "We'll roast wieners if anybody's hungry."

Shoot, I was always hungry, so that sounded mighty good to me. It had gotten dark while we were eating our hot dogs. When we finished, Uncle Ben told Franklin to go get the paper sack out of the car. Franklin ran to get it and started pulling out what would help us celebrate. It was a big bag of fireworks. Uncle Ben said, "Now, Franklin, since you're the oldest, you can help light matches for these things, but you have to be particular." Franklin told him that he would be. I wasn't sure, but it looked like Franklin stood up a little bit taller when Uncle Ben told him that.

Franklin had a flashlight and he would read the names of the different stuff before he lit it. He started out with little firecrackers called Daisy Pops. Then he got out a cherry bomb. He said, "Stop up your ears. This is a loud one!" B - O - O - M!

It was loud, even with each of my pointing fingers in my ears. Then he lit a bunch of Black Cat firecrackers. He pulled out a Bottle Rocket. He lit it and sent it way up. When it exploded, it shot off reds and blues and greens in every direction. Ida Claire said that that was the one that she liked the best. Franklin took out an M-80.

He told us that it was louder than the cherry bomb. Aunt Ima said, "I hope it doesn't make us go deaf." We all put our fingers in our ears for that one.

Finally, Uncle Ben said that we needed to get things together and head for home. Franklin said that there were some sparklers left in the sack. Uncle Ben told him that those could be done at home since they didn't make too much noise. But, he said, "Y'all be sure to do those outside, not in the house." We all told him that we would.

On the way home I almost fell asleep. Ida Claire was sleepy, too. When we turned in at the house, Ida Claire said, "We really did do a good job of celebrating July 4th, didn't we?" Everybody in the car nodded and smiled a little smile.

Chapter 12

This Is The House That We Built

Three buildings were in a row across the street in the next block. One building was an old empty house. Another was a house that belonged to a woman with grown-up children. And the third building was a place of business. Lots of ladies went to work there five days a week. It had some company name but we just called it the shirt factory (because shirts were made there). We probably wouldn't have been too interested with any kind of factory, except, some days when big trucks came, it made a difference to us. These trucks brought boxes to the back door of the factory. After the factory workers unloaded the stuff in the boxes, they put them in a big wooden fenced area in back of the factory. Then, the boxes seemed to be just trash to everybody. But they were not trash to Ida Claire and me.

Early in the morning I went to see what Ida Claire wanted to play. She said, "I know, Will, let's ask if we can go to the shirt factory to get some boxes." We both ran to ask Aunt Ima. She said that it would be okay, but we needed to check with Sophie first. Sophie was my Mama's name. So we ran back to my house.

Ida Claire said to me, "Let me do the talking, Will. Aunt Sophie will usually let us do stuff when I ask." I just nodded because we had gotten to the back door then. Ida Claire said, "Aunt Sophie, Mama said it was alright with her for us to go get some boxes at the shirt factory. But, she said for Will and me to come ask you first. So, is it alright with you, too?"

Mama nodded and then she said, "Y'all watch for cars when you're crossing the street. And let me know when y'all get back so I'll know where you are!" We barely heard her last words because we had already started out the door. We got to the curb and looked both ways. Nothing was coming on the side street, so we crossed. Then we walked to the corner. We had to look both ways on the other street. One car was coming, so we waited. I asked Ida Claire why we just couldn't cross at the corner and go from one corner to the other. She told me that that was called jay-walking and that it was dangerous and against the law. She said that she had learned that last year in school. I didn't say anything, but I thought I was going to have a lot of new things to learn when I got to school. I sure hoped that I was smart enough and not slow-to-learn like Dewey. Ida Claire must have read my mind. "It won't be long, Will, until you're in school and you'll be learning all sorts of good stuff. It will be fun, too."

We were at the wooden fence spot in back of the factory in just a few minutes. It looked like we had some new, crisp card-board boxes to choose from. Ida Claire reached over and pulled on one of the big ones. "Look, Will, this one looks pretty good to use. You climb over the wooden boards and hold it up and I'll pull it over." We both took a deep breath. Cardboard boxes from the shirt factory always had that particular smell. Franklin had told us it was the cloth that was shipped in the boxes that made them smell that way. I don't know how he knew stuff like that, but he sure was smart. Anyway, we found four boxes that looked pretty good. One was really big. We found another one almost that same size, but it had a rip on one corner. So, we left it. Two of the oth-ers were almost the same size. They were big enough to be two rooms in the house. And the other one was even bigger than those two. We put all of the smaller ones into the largest box. Then Ida Claire grabbed hold of a flap on the box and said, "I'll pull to start with and you push, Will." It didn't matter who did what because halfway home we would swap places anyway. While the boxes were on the little brown gravel, they would almost roll along. But, on the pavement we scrubbed them towards home. We finally made it to the curb. By this time I was pulling and Ida Claire was pushing. She came around to where I was and helped me lift the boxes over the curb. Then we were on the grass and clover, so the boxes would slide pretty good. We pushed them to the shade under the cherry laurel trees.

Now, the fun part would really begin. We had to decide which way the boxes would be connected. First, we took all the smaller boxes out of the big one. Of course, the big one would be the main room in the house. We decided to let it be on one end. We would use the two smaller ones as a tunnel hall to get to the biggest room. Then we decided to turn one of the boxes upside down on top of the big one. That way it looked like we had a two-story house. Really, we would be able to stand up straight in that section of our cardboard house after a hole was cut in the top of the big box.

We went in the house to see if Franklin would use his pocketknife to cut some windows and doors for us. Ida Claire asked Aunt Ima where Franklin was because we didn't see him. She said that he had gone down to the field with some bigger boys. She asked us what we wanted. We told her. She said that she was busy right then, but she could cut the windows and doors for us with a paring knife in just a little while. She told us to draw where we wanted the openings and she would cut them. So we went and got a pencil and marked the places for the windows and doors. We waited just a few more minutes and Aunt Ima came to cut the openings for us. We started in the tunnel at one end. Ida Claire reminded me to brush off my feet good. She didn't like to sit on grit. Shoot, I didn't either. We pushed back one of the window flaps and that let in a nice little breeze. It felt nice and cool and smooth in our cardboard house. And the gnats didn't bother us in there either. While we were resting, I asked Ida Claire to tell me one of the good stories she heard at school last year. She asked me if I knew why a rabbit wiggles his nose. I told her that I didn't. Then Ida Claire told this story:

"A long time ago there was a little rabbit that lived in a thicket. Now, this rabbit didn't look like rabbits do now. No, this little rabbit had short, fat ears and short, fat feet, and he didn't have whiskers. But, this rabbit made a squeaky sound with his nose every time he talked. Mother Rabbit got tired of the squeaky noise that Little Rabbit made. She told Little Rabbit to go ask Wise Old Owl if he knew what Little Rabbit could do to stop that squeaking. So, Little Rabbit started on his trip to Owl's tree.

On the way there he saw many other animals. Each one he saw had a good idea to help him stop his squeaking. First, the monkey said that he knew what to do to stop that squeaking. He grabbed Little Rabbit by his short, fat ears. And, he began to shake him. The monkey thought that he could shake the squeak out of Rabbit. But, the only thing he did was make the poor little rabbit's short, fat ears become long, floppy ears. Little Rabbit was disappointed, but he walked on towards Owl's tree.

Next, he meet a fox. The fox told him that he had a great idea to stop the squeak. But, Little Rabbit would need to go into his den to hear the idea. Little Rabbit was not that crazy. He knew that if he followed the fox into his den, that the fox would eat him alive for sure. So, Little Rabbit dug his hind paws into the ground but the fox tried to get him anyway. He grabbed Rabbit's front paws and pulled with all his might. Unfortunately, the fox pulled too hard and Rabbit's feet stretched and stretched and grew longer and thinner. The fox's paws slipped and he started rolling backwards and went rolling into his den.

Poor Little Rabbit hopped off flippity-floppity still headed towards Wise Owl's tree. He had begun to cry. A little bird came down and tried to wipe away his tears. But, he did not do just that. By accident, he also pulled some of Little Rabbit's hair under his nose. A few strands of hair stuck straight out just like whiskers.

The next animal that Rabbit saw was a beaver by a pond. The beaver listened to the story that Little Rabbit told him. He told Little Rabbit that he thought he could help him. The beaver was planning to use his big flat tail. He was pretending to hit Rabbit in the face with his tail, and he thought that would scare the squeaking sound out of Rabbit. But, instead, the beaver's tail smacked Little Rabbit right in the nose. It turned pink instead of black.

Little Rabbit finally reached Wise Owl's tree. Wise Owl almost didn't recognize Little Rabbit. But, when Rabbit started to talk, Owl heard that squeak and knew who it was. Little Rabbit told him that it wasn't worth all the torture that he had gone through just because of his squeaky talk. So, he decided to just not talk, and instead just wiggle his nose. Wise Owl told him that that sounded wise to him. And, since that day, no rabbits have talked or squeaked, they just wiggle their noses!"

I clapped when Ida Claire finished her story. We were looking through the top cracks of the cardboard box at the pretty white clouds. Ida Claire asked what I wanted to do now. Before I could answer we heard someone calling, "Ida Claire, Will, where are y'all? What are you doing? Do you want to play something?" We looked out of our house and there stood Millie. Now, we would have something new to play. We didn't know what, but we knew it would be fun.

Chapter 13

Smiling In Heaven

Three flat stones and a piece of chalk were in the palm of Millie's hand when she opened it to show us what she had. Millie lived down the street about eight houses across the road. She had been in Ida Claire's class at school for the past two years. As a matter of fact, they had been friends since they were two years old. Millie is the one that taught Ida Claire to pump in the swings to keep her swinging without anybody pushing. And after Ida Claire learned, she taught me how to pump, too. We usually played with her a lot, but she hadn't been home very much lately. She said that she had been visiting her cousin in Texas. She had been gone for three weeks. I didn't know where this Texas place was, but it must have been a pretty good ways from where we lived. Anyway, she told us that those stones in her hand came from Texas. And, she thought they would make good hopscotch markers. She asked us if we wanted to play. Ida Claire asked her if she wanted to come into our house first. So, she went to the other end of the tunnel hall, brushed off her feet, and came in. Millie sniffed and said, "Nothing else smells like a new cardboard house, does it?" We grinned and nodded. She asked if we were ready to play hopscotch. We told her that we were.

We all climbed out of the cardboard house. Millie asked, "Do you want me to draw it on the sidewalk or in the dirt? I brought a piece of chalk if you want it on the sidewalk." I told them that I liked it on the dirt better. I had a stick that was good for dirt drawing, and I told Millie that she could use it. It had been a long time since we had played hopscotch, so I asked Ida Claire to explain the rules again.

So, Ida Claire explained the game of hopscotch. She said that it was one of the games that they played a lot at recess in school last year. "You have to draw your boxes just right first. You should have three in a row then two side by side. Next, will be one box then another double. At the top of the drawing you need one more box, then a circle. That circle is called heaven. You have to remember not to show your teeth in heaven. If you do, you have to go back to the beginning. Each box has a number in it. You take turns throwing your own rock to a box and work your way up to heaven, starting at box one. You have to jump or hop on just one foot and pick up your rock when you come to it then hop back to the start. If you don't step on lines or in any box that has a rock, then you can keep going until you mess up. If you mess up, it's the next person's turn. The winner is the first one to get to heaven. Do you remember the game, Will?"

I told her that I did. I said, "I remember that rule about heaven, too. I know that you're not supposed to show your teeth or talk or laugh or anything." I asked Ida Claire if she remembered that time that Dewey made me mess up after I had made it all the way to heaven. Ida Claire nodded and grinned. Millie wanted to know how Dewey made me mess up. I told her that while I was in the heaven circle, Dewey made a noise that wasn't very nice. He put his hand up under his arm and squeezed down. I told her I got tickled and showed my teeth and laughed out loud. So, I had to start over. Millie said that Dewey was pretty bad all right.

Millie said for us to put out our fists and she would see who would go first by counting potatoes. I had both of mine ready, Ida Claire was next, then Millie. Millie would hit each fist when she counted, "One potato, two potatoes, three potatoes, four; five potatoes, six potatoes, seven potatoes, more." I had to put one hand behind my back. Then she started counting the next fist. She went around again. This time one of Millie's own fists had to be moved behind her back. Ida Claire was the last one to lose one of her potato fists. She said that she knew she would get to be the first at hopscotch. I don't know how she knew that because Millie wasn't even through counting yet. But, sure enough, Ida Claire was the last one to have a potato fist out, so she was the winner. I reckon she had counted more potatoes than I had.

Millie said that she wanted the blue rock to be her marker, and that we could choose between the other two. One was green and other one was brown. I knew that Ida Claire liked green the best, so I said that I would use the brown one. It didn't really matter to me too much because hopscotch wasn't my favorite game. It was kinda hard to do all that hopping on just one foot. But, Ida Claire said that it was good to practice and it would help my balance. She started by throwing her marker into box one. It was always easy to get one, two, and three. But, one time, I had tried to use a round rock and it rolled out of the box every time. Anyway, we kept playing and taking turns. I was trying to do my best, and I was really practicing my balancing, I thought. I had made it all the way up to box nine. It sure was a good thing there was a rule about being able to put your other hand on the ground to help keep your balance. All I had to say was "Butterfingers". And I said it a lot!

While we were playing, Franklin came walking up with a bow and arrow in his hand. He had been down at the field with the bigger boys. Ida Claire and I couldn't go to the field by ourselves. Aunt Ima and Mama wouldn't let us. The only time we got to go to the field was on kite-flying day. One day every year when it was really windy, Daddy would take us there to fly a kite that he had made. Boy, that was some kinda fun. Anyway, while Ida Claire was hopping, Franklin told us about his bow and arrow he made. He said that he had cut a limb off a chinaberry tree. Then, he had trimmed the little branches off and bent it in the shape of a bow. He tied a string around both ends and had a really good bow made without too much trouble. Then, he got a smaller branch and stripped it to be his arrow. He said that he came home to get a bottle cap to smash together for the point on the arrow. He told me that I was really too little to shoot it though. And then it was my turn at hopscotch again.

I hopped up the boxes just right. I had to be careful not to step into any box that had Ida Claire's or Millie's marker in it. Then, I had finally made it to heaven. I was having to really think hard about it so I wouldn't show my teeth and laugh. All of a sudden, Franklin said, "Hey, Squirt, do you want to hold my bow?"

Before I could think about the rule, I said, "Shoot, yeah!" I just plain forgot about not being able to talk in heaven. Millie and Ida Claire reminded me in a hurry though. So, I had to start over. Oh, well, I at least got to see Frankin's bow and hold it. Millie and Ida Claire decided that they would call it a tie, and they quit playing, too.

Aunt Ima came outside to see what we were doing. She told Franklin not to shoot that arrow towards anybody. She said, "You need to be mighty careful or you'll put somebody's eye out." Franklin told her that they would be shooting towards a target and trying to hit the bull's eye. And, he started walking back down to the field. I wished that I was old enough to go to the field that day for sure. Then, Millie said that she had another idea of something fun to play. Ida Claire and I looked at each other, then we looked at Millie. It was about middle of the afternoon now, and we knew we had time for some more fun.

Chapter 14

War Is A Berry Serious Business

Three ideas were mentioned by Millie for us to choose which one to play next. Since we still had the hopscotch markers from Texas, we decided we could play rock school. We went to my house for this. My front porch had five concrete steps leading up to it. So that gave us grades one through five. Ida Claire and I didn't know the rules to this game. Millie had played this at her cousin's house when she was visiting in Texas. She said that she would be the teacher first. Then she started telling us how to play. "Everybody starts out in first grade. That will be the bottom step. I will have my hands behind me and the rock will be in one fist. When it's your turn, I'll put my two fists in front of you. You will get to pick one of them. If you pick the one that has the rock, then I'll ask you a question. If you can answer the question right, then, you'll get to go up to the next step or grade. Then, it's the next person's turn. The first one to make it to the top will get to be the teacher next. Do y'all understand the rules okay?"

Ida Claire nodded. But, I asked, "What if the questions are too hard and I don't know the right answer? Then, what will I do?"

Millie said, "Well, you'll just stay where you are in that same grade until next time. But, don't worry, I'll be lenient on you!" I hoped that was something good and not bad. I sure did have a lot to learn when I got to school. Ida Claire whispered that lenient meant that Millie would ask sorta easy questions. Then, Millie said, "Okay, Will, pick a fist." I chose the one that had the rock in it. But I didn't know whether to be happy or not about it. Millie asked, "Will, can you spell 'cat'?"

I said, "Shoot, yeah, anybody can spell 'cat' - c - a - t." Whew! I was glad that Ida Claire had taught me that word.

Millie told me that I passed to second grade, so I could move up a step. Then Millie put both fists behind her again. This time it was Ida Claire's turn. She picked the right fist, too. Millie asked her if she knew how to make thirty cents. Ida Claire told her that that was easy: It took three dimes to make thirty cents. I even knew that one because of the green ring that Ida Claire bought at the dime store. Then, Ida Claire passed to second grade, too.

It was my turn again, but I guessed the fist that didn't have the rock in it. So, I had to stay in the same grade. Millie moved back to Ida Claire. Ida Claire picked the fist with the rock again. Millie asked her what the sum of fifteen and fifteen was. Ida Claire waited a minute and then said the answer thirty. Millie told her that was right and to go up to the next grade. Whew! It's a good thing that I didn't get that question. I wasn't sure what sum was, much less the answer thirty. We kept playing. Ida Claire had gotten up to fourth grade when we saw Franklin and the two boys coming up to the house.

Franklin said, "What are y'all playing?" Ida Claire and I looked at each other. I was wondering what Franklin wanted because usually he didn't want to play anywhere close to us if the big boys were around. Millie told him that we were playing "rock school". She showed him the rocks that she had brought back from Texas. Oscar and Henry, the two big boys with Franklin, looked at the rocks, too. Then, Franklin said, "I was just wondering if you're through with your cardboard box house."

I looked at Ida Claire. She said, "I don't know. Why are you asking?" Franklin told her that if we were through with the boxes, then they might could use them for forts. Ida Claire looked at me. I nodded that that would be okay with me.

Ida Claire said, "Franklin, you know that Mama won't let you shoot that bow and arrow at anybody. And, anyway, we might want to use the boxes later. Why don't y'all go to get some more boxes down at the shirt factory?" Franklin told her that they would be using pea shooters, not the arrows. And he said that they had thought about going to get their own boxes from the shirt factory, but it seemed like a waste of time. Then, he told us that if he could use the boxes, he would let us sit in the one that would be his fort. Well, that sounded good to us. So, Ida Claire said, "All right! Where do you want the boxes to be moved?"

While Franklin, Oscar, and Henry started towards the boxes, I ran into the house. I had to dig in my toy chest. But, thank goodness, I found my pea shooter in a hurry. It was orange with yellow stripes. Ida Claire and Millie ran to get Ida Claire's out of her house. I even found another pea shooter. It was red with white stripes. I must have liked that one because it reminded me of peppermint candy. By the time I got outside, Ida Claire and Millie were coming out of the house. Ida Claire asked, "Did you find an extra one, Will? The only one I found was my purple and green one." I held up the two I had and Millie shouted. I guess that she really wanted to play fort, too. Before we started across the yard, Ida Claire told us to get some nandina berries off the bush at the corner of the porch. All three of us got two handfuls. We got all the berries we could and poked then down into our pockets. Ida Claire reminded us to not swallow the berries because they might be poisonous.

When we got to Franklin's box fort, he had out his pocketknife. He was cutting a little hole the size of the knife blade. He was turning the blade around and around to make a good hole. Then, up above each pea shooter hole, he made a slit to look out of. This slit was as wide as a person's head. He made it only high enough to see out of but not too big to let a berry come in. He told us that if we would be good fighters that we could be soldiers in his army. Shoot, I would be the best soldier that Franklin ever did see. He asked us if we had gotten any berries yet. All three of us showed him our pockets. He looked at me and told me to go find some more ammunition. He said that I would have time before the first battle of the war. So, I took off and went into the kitchen. I asked Mama if she had any little dried peas in a bag. While she reached up in the cabinet, she asked me what they were for. I told her that we needed the ammunition so we could win the war. She said, "Oh." She gave me half a bag and then she smiled. I don't know why she smiled. This war was serious business!

Franklin had our box fort up above the ditch next to the mimosa tree. Oscar had his box fort along the edge of the ditch next to the crape myrtle. And Henry put his fort down in the ditch. It was sorta close to the street. Franklin said that we definitely had the advantage. He acted proud of that; so I was, too. Oscar asked if anybody had a surrender flag. Nobody had thought about that. So, Franklin told Ida Claire to go get three of Uncle Ben's white handkerchiefs. She came back and gave one to Oscar, one to Henry, and we kept one. We weren't gonna need it though. I knew if you waved that white flag, that meant that you gave up. And I knew that Franklin didn't give up on anything. Franklin told me to go get two pine cones. I asked, "What will those be for, Franklin?" He kinda grinned and told me that they would make good hand grenades.

When everybody was situated in their forts, Oscar said, "I declare war, let the battles begin." Henry did the same. Then, Franklin did. Ida Claire, Millie, and I just yelled as loud as we could. Franklin told us that we didn't have to be so loud. Because, inside that box all the noise bounces off the walls, and it might make him go deaf. We each put a berry and a pea shooter in our mouth and fired out the little openings. Ida Claire and Millie were shooting at Oscar's fort. And, Franklin and I were firing on Henry's. Franklin said that the action was heated, but we were holding our own. I could hear the berries bounce off the side of our cardboard fort wall. I was glad to be inside because if a berry hit you, it would really sting. Then Franklin told me to bring out the heavy ammo. I just waited for him to tell me just exactly what the heavy ammo really was. He motioned to the pine cones. Then, he told me to sneak out the back of the fort and loft it over to Henry's fort. I was about to get sweaty; so I was glad to get to step outside for just a minute. But, about the time I started to push the back flap open, Franklin whispered for me to freeze. He waved for me to come look out my peep hole. Since we were higher up, we could see exactly what was happening.

Oscar must have been ready to end the war. The best we could tell was that he had a mouthful of berries and had unloaded them towards Henry's fort. He had so many berries that he overshot his mark. And, that would have been fine, except, a car was coming by at the same time. And, the berries spattered the windshield of the car. And, what made it worse was that it was a black and white police car. And, what made it even worse was that the car stopped and the policeman got out. Franklin whispered for us to stay quiet and to stay in the box. Shoot, he didn't have to worry about us going anywhere; we were glued to the spot. Franklin walked out. Oscar and Henry came out of their boxes, too. We heard the policeman tell them to be more careful and not to play so close to the street. I was mighty glad that Franklin told us to stay in the box. And he sure didn't have to worry about us saying a word. When I looked at Ida Claire, she was biting her fingernails. And when I looked at Millie, she was waving that white surrender handkerchief just as hard as she could!

Chapter 15

That's The Way The Ball Bounces

Three bags of groceries were in the car trunk for Aunt Ima. And there were two bags of groceries that were Mama's. It was Thursday morning and we had just gotten back from the Colonial store. Every Thursday Aunt Ima, Grandmama, Mama, Ida Claire, and I would get in Uncle Ben's blue and white car to go buy groceries. Ida Claire would get to push a grocery buggy. But, Aunt Ima would get mighty upset if Ida Claire bumped into her. Mama let me try to push her buggy one time, but only one time. That thing just had a mind of its own. Mama said she didn't want to buy broken jars of stuff because we sure couldn't eat 'em. I don't know why she said that because I wasn't going to put the broken ones I knocked off the shelf into our buggy.

We helped to take the groceries into the house. Aunt Ima said that we could each get some orange circus peanuts candy to take outside and eat while we were playing. I really liked orange peanuts. Of course, I liked anything orange. When we got outside, Ida Claire said, "I reckon we've gotten the good out of the cardboard boxes the way they are now. After all, we've had a mighty nice house and a really good fort." I nodded. Then, I smiled because I remembered what we did with the boxes the last time we got some. Ida Claire asked, "Well, are you ready to stack them in a pile?"

I told her, "Shoot, yeah, let's climb our box mountain." We put the biggest on the bottom in the middle of a patch of clover. Then, we put the next size on top of that. Just using those two boxes made a mountain taller that we were. Then, Ida Claire started climbing up one side and I climbed up the other. These boxes were pretty sturdy until we started jumping. Each jump made the cardboard "give" just a little. We felt and heard the corners start to give away and then we plopped down just as hard as we could. We both threw our heads back and laughed hard. The boxes were beginning to squoosh and get flatter. So we got another box and put it on top and did the same thing about jumping and plopping. Then we got the last one. On this one we got a running start and jumped up and landed flat down on it. Millie came in the yard about the time we made our last jump.

She said, "It looks like y'all are getting ready to make a great slide." She had been in our yard before when we were playing on our cardboard slide. We told her that we sure were and asked her if she wanted to help us get it ready. I drug one of the flattened boxes to the lowest dip in my front yard. We flattened the box out even more. Then, we covered about half of that box with the next box. Then, on the top half of that flattened box, we put the other one. All of the flattened cardboard was slanting downhill just a little. When we finished getting all of the cardboard laid out, it was about as wide as a car and about as long as two cars put together. Then, we took the last box and tore it into little flat pieces that we could hold on to when we slid. I usually put the flat cardboard piece on my back side. Ida Claire told me to go first if I wanted to. Shoot, this was as fun as building the house and playing fort. I started at the top of the yard and ran as fast as I could. Ida Claire and Millie were on each side of the cardboard slide. They were holding the pieces so they would stay spread out and not bunch together. When I got to the slide, I put that flat piece on my back. Then, I jumped up and kept my feet in the air. My cardboard piece under my back side made me slip along pretty fast. Then, it was Millie's turn. She usually would run and land on her stomach to slide. She used the cardboard flat piece, too, because it always made it faster. She had to be sure to keep her head up good though. Ida Claire and I were on the sides holding the main slide in place. When it was Ida Claire's turn, she said that she wanted to try a new way. So, she put the cardboard flat piece on the sliding part at the top first. She wasn't holding it like we usually did. She took off running and landed on her knees. She really slid! She told us that she thought that was the best way so far. So, of course, Millie and I wanted to try it. But, about the time I started running, it started raining. We had been so busy having fun, we didn't notice the dark clouds in the sky. Mama stuck her head out the door and told us to clean up the boxes because the rain would ruin them anyway. She said that it would be raining cats and dogs pretty soon, and we might get drenched. So, the three of us started dragging the cardboard to the curb. That way the trash truck could pick it up on Saturday.

Since it was raining so hard, Millie couldn't go back home yet. We decided we would all go to Ida Claire's house and find something that we could play. Millie asked if we had played jackstones lately. We told her that we hadn't. She said that she had learned a whole new round to do with jackstones while she was playing with her cousin in Texas last week. Ida Claire asked her if it was very hard to play. Millie told her that it was at first, but she knew that with some practice, she would be able to do it without any trouble. She didn't mention that she thought that I would be able to do it without any trouble. Of course, I had trouble with the easiest part of jackstones, much less a whole new round. It seemed that it was always my turn when that ball wanted to go haywire. It would always take a crazy bounce like it was in a hurry to go play somewhere else.

Millie said that she would count potatoes and told us to put out our fists. This time she got to start the game. She started the game picking up "one-zies". That was the easiest of all. I could even do that one pretty good. But she had to be careful to pick up only one jack and not touch any of the others. If she did, she would lose her turn. Then, she went to "two-zies", "three-zies", and all the way to "ten-zies". When she got to "ten-zies", she threw the jacks up then turned her hand over under the jacks. All the jacks that fell on top of her hand counted like she had already picked them up. It was important not to scatter them too much, if possible. If I ever made it to "nine-zies", I would just sorta set the handful of jackstones down in one place. I knew if I scattered them too much, I never would pick them up in one hand. That was hard enough. But, watching the ball and grabbing it after it had bounced just one time was really tough. Millie and Ida Claire did pretty good on the first round. Shoot, I made it to "eight-zies". And that was pretty good for me. I really thought that jackstones were sissy. But, every now and then, if Franklin was bored, he would even play. He told me that it really took good eye-hand coordination and that would help me with my baseball game. I didn't know what that eye-hand thing was he was talking about, and I sure didn't see how a tiny rubber ball had anything to do with a hard baseball. But, I knew Franklin was smart, so I tried to be good at jackstones.

Millie and Ida Claire left me in round one for a long time. They did "in the cave" for the next round. I liked that one because you could make a little cave on the floor with one hand and scoop the jacks along the floor in a quick motion, then, catch the ball after it bounced. They both finished that round. I had decided I would just be stuck on "eight-zies". The next round they did was "in the basket". In this round they had to pick up the jacks, put them in the other hand, then, catch the ball after it bounced. Then, Millie explained the new round she had learned. It was called "around the world". She said that the ball had to bounce twice. That sounded good to me. Millie threw the ball up a little bit higher than usual. She picked up the jack, circled around the ball, let it bounce again, and then caught the ball. Ida Claire said that she could see why that would take a lot of practice.

It was finally my turn again. I was still on "eight-zies". I threw the ball up higher than usual. It came down and bounced on top of one of the left over jackstones. The jack scooted out one way and the ball scooted under the heater. I started to reach up under the heater to get it. Millie asked me why I didn't just leave the ball under the heater and that way we would know where it was for the next time. We all laughed. The telephone rang. The call was Millie's Mama. She told Millie to come home since the rain had slacked up some. We told each other bye. Ida Claire said that we better make sure to clean up good. She said to double check. Because, one time Uncle Ben stepped on one of those jackstones that was left on the floor. And he was barefooted. She said that he really fussed about it. And he told her if he ever saw another one left on the floor, that he would put it in the garbage can.

Ida Claire and I talked about what we might play next. But, Mama hollered out the back door for me to come home because supper was ready. I had been so busy watching Ida Claire and Millie go "in the cave" and "around the world" that I had forgotten about eating. But, all of a sudden, I was just about to starve.

Chapter 16

"Attention, Draw Swords!"

Three days later was Sunday. Early that morning I went over to Ida Claire's house to see if I still could go to Sunday School and church with her that day. I usually went to the Methodist Church. But, she had asked Mama early in the week if it would be okay for me to go to the Baptist Church with her. It was the beginning day for Vacation Bible School week. They called it Kick-Off Sunday. When I got to Aunt Ima's, the TV was going strong. Different gospel groups were singing their hearts out. Aunt Ima kept that TV on gospel singing on Sunday from the time she got up until their family left to go to Sunday School. Ida Claire was finishing her toast and tea that she had for breakfast. Ida Claire asked me what I was planning to wear. "I wish I could just wear my shorts. But Mama laid out a white shirt and my blue bow tie. I reckon that thing will just about choke me to death," I told Ida Claire.

She said, "Well, just be glad that you don't have to wear a scratchy, lacy petticoat under a dress. I just about itch too death every Sunday." Aunt Ima heard what she said. But she told her that it didn't hurt her to look like a little girl one day out of the week. Ida Claire just said, "Yes, ma'am" to that. After I thought about that scratchy petticoat, I decided maybe my bow tie wasn't so bad after all.

When we got to Sunday School, I went to Ida Claire's class with her. I really was too little to be in the junior class. But, since I was a visitor, the teacher let me stay. Ida Claire told me that she was in the primary class like me last year. She said that she would stay in the junior class until she got promoted to the intermediate. That was Franklin's age group. All three of these groups meet together first for what they called assembly. A man named Mr.

Booth stood at the front and gave the devotional. He talked about how the Bible tells us to tithe our money. I looked at Ida Claire. I didn't know what he was talking about. She whispered, "He's talking about giving some of your money to Sunday School every Sunday." Mr. Booth went on to tell all the boys and girls that he always told his children to give part of their allowance to Jesus first. He said that it really belongs to Jesus anyway and you should always be a cheerful giver. He said that one Sunday his youngest son decided to keep his whole fifty cents that he had gotten for allowance that week. And he didn't give the nickel he was supposed to give to church. His son didn't feel bad because he was planning to buy something that cost exactly fifty cents the next Saturday.. He had put his money in a safe place. When it came time to go to town the next Saturday, he counted his money. And five cents of that money was missing. That's the amount he should have given to the church for his tithe. Mr. Booth said that it was a mystery, but he told his son that you should never try to rob God from what is rightfully His.

We left the assembly and went to the three regular classes. In the junior class, Ida Claire was the secretary. It was her job to do the attendance. The teacher was Mrs. Booth. She told Ida Claire to check to see who was present. My ears perked up. I didn't know that we might get a present. But Ida Claire just said the children's names, and they said, "Here". Then, she asked how many had brought their Bibles. So, that was why she stuck that Bible in my hand right before we got into the car this morning! She wanted to know next if we had any offering. I saw Billy reach into his pocket. After Mr. Booth's talk, I was glad Mama had given me a dime before we left home. I was cheerful, too, when I gave it to Ida Claire. I smiled a big smile. Shoot, I sure didn't want to lose any money.

Mrs. Booth said that we would have sentence prayers before she started the lesson. She asked that anyone that wanted to, could say a prayer. Almost all of the girls said a prayer. And two of the boys said something. I was trying hard not to peek, but I just had to a little, because I didn't know who was talking. I did know that I wasn't going to say anything though. Mrs. Booth asked who had studied their lesson for Sunday School. When I looked around, the same boys and girls that said the prayers were the ones that raised their hands. Mrs. Booth said that the lesson was about telling the truth and how we must always be honest. She said that sometimes people think it's alright to tell just a little white lie, but it's not! A little white lie can grow into a big, horrible lie. She told us that she remembered her Grandpa telling her something when she was a little girl. And she knew that she would never forget it. He told her that "I Heard" and "They Say" were the two biggest liars in the world. And that was something that we needed to remember always. I didn't know who she was talking about, but I was pretty sure that I had never met either one of them before.

She finished the lesson and said that we had a little time left before the bell rang. Some of the children wanted to do a Bible drill. I never had done this before, so I just sat and watched. Billy just watched, too. The kids stood up, holding their Bibles by their side. Mrs. Booth said, "Attention, draw swords, John 3:16, charge!" Whew! All of the boys and girls started flipping through their Bibles. That's when I found out that a Bible drill is like a Bible race. I would have to remember to ask Ida Claire about the "draw swords" part. Then, the bell rang. We went in to the big church next.

We sat on the same pew with Aunt Ima and Uncle Ben. The preacher announced about the times of Vacation Bible School for the week. I wasn't too worried about that because I knew that Ida Claire would tell me when to go with her to church every day. I couldn't tell time, yet, anyway. Then, the preacher welcomed the visitors and told them to stand. Ida Claire motioned for me to stand up. Everybody looked at me and smiled. I sure did feel mighty hot all of a sudden and my bow tie really choked me then. But, I tried to smile back at the folks.

I really liked the singing part that we did next. The man in front said for us to turn to page 357 in our hymnals. I didn't know that big number. I wasn't even sure I would learn up to that high in first grade. But Ida Claire found it. He said that we would be singing, "Bringing in the Sheets." I thought that I might have not heard that exactly right. I didn't know what sheets had to do with church. So, I listened closely to see if I had gotten confused. In the song everybody was singing the same. It sounded like they were saying: "Bringing in the sheets, bringing in the sheets, we shall come with Georgia, bringing in the sheets." So, the next time we got to that part, I sang just like everybody else! I never had sung that song at my church, but I liked it. I reckon whoever wrote that song liked to go with somebody named Georgia when she brought the sheets in off the clothesline.

The preacher talked next. He talked about a little man named Zaccheus. He read from the Bible about how Zaccheus wanted to see Jesus, but he was just too short to see over the crowd. So, he ran ahead and climbed up in a sycamore tree. I liked that story because I loved to climb trees, too. The preacher was really preaching, but, about that time I looked up and saw a wasp flying around in the ceiling. Then, I started thinking about how we could climb the mimosa tree to catch bumblebees. And, the next thing I knew, Ida Claire was punching me, telling me to wake up. The preacher said for everybody to stand so we could sing the last song of the morning. Shoot, I had heard and learned so many new things, it was hard to believe it was still just morning. While the preacher was praying, I was thinking which one to ask Ida Claire about first. I had decided that first I would ask about the song that was talking about "sheets". Then, I heard the preacher say, "Amen".

Chapter 17

Stepping Up To High Places

Three planks were in Franklin's arms. Ida Claire had a hammer and a fistful of nails. It was Sunday afternoon and Franklin had plans for a tree house. On the way home from church that day, he had asked Uncle Ben if he had any old boards that we might could use. I wondered why he didn't just come right out and ask Uncle Ben whether we could build a tree house or not. I asked Franklin about that after dinner. He said, "Well, Squirt, sometimes you just have to test the waters before you jump in with both feet. You see, grown-ups don't always like a straight-out question. You might have to lead them into knowing what you're talking about." But Franklin had a sneaky grin on his face, and he stood up just a little bit taller.

I said, "Oh - h!" But I wasn't really sure what he was talking about. I reckon I could use what he said later. I thought that maybe the next time I went fishing with Daddy maybe I could ask about jumping in the water like Franklin said. Anyway, Franklin had found out that we could make a tree house in the mimosa tree that was growing right beside the marble holes. So, Franklin said to Ida Claire and me, "Y'all go to see if there might be some scrap lumber in the back next to the gas tank. There might be some under the drum." We knew exactly where Franklin meant because lots of times we put a towel over that drum, and it became our horse when we were playing cowboys. We could swing up over that drum and straddle it just like it was a real horse. We would have a rope tied to the gas pump handle in front and tell him to "Giddy-up". He really didn't ever move or even have a head except in our imagination. But, we played a lot, and so we galloped a heap of miles on the gas-drum horse.

We did find some more boards that we could use for the tree house. Franklin told us to pile them at the bottom of the tree. He started arranging them from longest to shortest. When he picked up one of the boards, a little brown lizard was crawling on it. He grabbed the lizard and said that he would be right back. We heard him call to Aunt Ima through the back screened door, "Mama, I have a lizard that I just caught. Do you want to see him?"

"Good gracious, sakes' alive, NO," Aunt Ima screamed. "You know I don't want to see that devilish thing. A lizard is too much like a snake!" Ida Claire and I grinned and Franklin had a sneaky grin on his face again.

"Mama, if you'll hand me a jar and some tin foil, you won't even have to see my new little pet." Aunt Ima opened the screened door in a hurry and stuck the jar and tin foil out to Franklin. He kept the lizard in one hand behind his back and took the jar with the other hand. I reckon he was afraid if he showed it to Aunt Ima that she would die of a heart attack. At least, that's what she always said.

Franklin put the lizard in the jar. Then, he put some grass in there with it. He took the tin foil and put it on the top of the jar and screwed the ring part of the lid down over the tin foil and the top of the jar. He took a little skinny twig and poked about five little holes in the top. Then he winked at us and said, "I reckon that ought to be a little safer than an ice pick." He looked at the lizard in the jar and said, "I have plans for you later." Then he sat the jar under the shade of the cherry laurel trees.

Franklin found six planks that were about the same length. He told us that he would nail them on the trunk of the tree and make it sorta like a ladder going up the tree. We didn't have any boards long enough to make a regular ladder. This mimosa tree had a long, thick trunk. It didn't branch out close to the ground like the one in the front yard did. Franklin said, "Come here, Will, and step up to show me how far your normal step is. I'll put the first plank just a little bit higher than that from the ground. Then, you and Ida Claire will only have to stretch a little to climb into this tree house." I thought that was mighty decent of Franklin. I reckon

Franklin didn't want to waste nails. So in each plank, he nailed just one nail right in the center of the plank and then into the tree. He nailed all of the planks on up to where the tree branched out. He stood on the ground to nail the first three planks. Then, he stood on the bottom plank to nail on the fourth. Then, he went to get his bicycle. He propped it on the trunk of the tree. He told us to hold it steady while he stood up on the seat of the bike and nailed in plank number five, and then six.

Franklin looked around and then he said, "We need something sturdy that we can use as a base while we put flooring in for the tree house, at least, to get started anyway. I know, we'll move the swing set over here. Y'all get on one end of the swings and I'll get at the other." So we slowly moved the swing set to sit under the tree for now. Ida Claire and I jumped up on the end bar and climbed on to the top while we held on to the tree branches. We didn't usually go up on top, but we did circus tricks on the end bar all the time. When we played circus, we would take turns swinging by the back of our knees with our heads hanging down until our faces turned red. On the end of the swing set where Franklin stood, the bar was bent just a little. I asked Ida Claire to tell me the story again of how the bar got bent.

Ida Claire had told the story plenty of times, so she knew it by heart. She said, "One day when you had gone fishing with your Daddy, we had some company. The lady had come to sell Avon stuff or something to Mama. She brought her daughter Bernice with her. Franklin and I were eating a banana Popsicle out on the swing set. The swing set was sorta new then. It was pretty. Its colors were bright red and green. I was sitting in one of the swings. And Franklin was up on one of the end bars. Bernice decided that she would get up on the other end bar."

Franklin added, "Yeah, she was too fat to sit in the swing! She thought that maybe the bar was wide enough for her, I reckon. And it was, but, when she got off, the bar was bent!"

I knew the answer to my next question, but I always asked it anyway when I heard the story about Bernice. "Franklin, you said that she was fat, but was she pretty?"

Franklin almost shouted, "Shoot, naw, she was mighty hard to favor. As a matter of fact, she was ugly as homemade sin!" We all laughed. So anytime I thought about that bent bar on the swing set, I thought about Bernice. Even though she was somebody I never had seen, I didn't really want to ever see her either.

Anyway, we had to get busy on the tree house flooring. So Ida Claire and I stood on the top bar while Franklin handed us each a board to put on the tree limbs. Then, he climbed up and hammered the boards down into the right place. We kept doing the same thing over and over and finally, we had a tree house. We moved the swing set back to the regular place. Franklin told us to climb back up to the tree house and he would throw a rope up to tie over a limb. He said that he planned to rig up a pulley for the rope and put a box on the bottom so we could haul stuff up to the tree house. Then, he went to get a string and the jar with the lizard in it. He put the jar in the box that was at the bottom of the pulley rope. Then, he climbed up the six planks to the top. He said that he would have to nail in some extra nails because some of the boards were already getting loose. "Y'all be sure to step in the center of each plank until I can get those planks nailed better."

Franklin took the lizard out of the jar and tied the string behind its front legs and around its body. He grinned at me and asked Ida Claire if she wanted a lizard necklace. Ida Claire told him, "Sure!" So he tied the string around her neck. She stiffened just a little, but she didn't jump or scream like most girls would have done. Ida Claire's shirt was green. That little lizard turned green, too. Franklin said that he was a chameleon and they change colors like that. He sure was smart.

We looked down from our tree house and saw Dewey at the bottom of the tree. "What are y'all d - d - do - ing up there?" he asked. We told him that we were just playing. Franklin grinned his sneaky grin.

Franklin said, "Come on up, Dewey, if you want to. Be sure to step on the outside edge of each board." So Dewey started climbing. He was barefooted as a yard dog. And Dewey was a little bit chunky.

He said, "S - S - Some of these b - b - boards are sorta w - w - wobbly, ain't they?" And about the time he stepped on the fourth plank, it was loose enough that it spun around. Then, his foot caught the end of each of the other planks all the way down to the ground. Each of those planks spun, too. So, Dewey hit the ground and the bottom four planks were pointing straight up. Ida Claire asked him if he was all right. Dewey was sitting on the ground laughing. So, we all started laughing, too. Dewey said, "Y - Y - Yeah, I'm f - f - fine, but you got to do some f - f -fixing if I'm gonna ever g - g - get to s - s - see your tree house!"

Chapter 18

What's In A Name?

Three tea cakes were on a napkin for each of us when we went to Grandmama's house the next day. We had been playing pitch with the baseball in the back alley. Grandmama's house was right behind mine. As a matter of fact, it was beside Dewey's family. It was about the middle of the afternoon and all of a sudden, I smelled something good cooking. Ida Claire and I both were sweating. I asked her if she was thirsty like I was. She said, "Yeah, let's go to Grandmama's and get some water. I bet that good smell is coming from her kitchen." Sure enough, the closer we got to Grandmama's kitchen, the stronger the good smell smelled. We opened the back screened door and walked right in. We never had to knock at Grandmama's house. Grandmama said that she thought that we might be thirsty and would probably enjoy a little snack. Yes, ma'am, those tea cakes looked like a perfect snack to us. She asked us if we wanted to drink lemonade or iced water. I told her that I wanted some good cold water. Daddy always said that nothing quenches your thirst like water. And, he kept a jug full of water in the refrigerator. He drank that water every night while he read the newspaper. Ida Claire said that she wanted lemonade. I knew that she would pick that because she even liked to suck raw lemons. Grandmama told us that she had saved each of us a little piece of cookie dough. She sat that on our napkin, too. We both loved cookie dough. As a matter of fact, Ida Claire even loved to eat raw biscuit dough. Aunt Ima always told her that it would give her worms, but she would save her some anyway. And we both really liked cake batter. We would always love if Mama, Aunt Ima, or Grandmama was making a cake. Ida Claire and I would each get a mixer beater to lick. And we would share cleaning the mixing bowl, too. Sometimes, we left that bowl so clean, I don't know why they thought it needed washing. It was as clean as a whistle.

While we were sitting at the table eating our tea cakes, Grandmama put a big button beside each of our napkins. Ida Claire's button was blue and mine was black. Grandmama went to the pantry and brought out some string and her scissors. She said, "Do y'all know how to make those buttons sing?"

Both of us looked at each other, raised our eyebrows, and then looked at Grandmama. We said, "No, ma'am!" Then, Grandmama showed us how to push the string through one of the holes in the middle of the button and then bring the string back through the second hole. She told us to tie both ends of the string together with a knot. Then, she used the scissors to cut the string at the end past the knot. Grandmama told us to place the circle of string around both hands and twirl it around and around so that it looked twisted in the middle where the button was.

"Now," she said, "bring your hands toward each other and then move them back out. You need to move your hands like you're trying to clap in slow motion. Listen, because you'll hear the button sing." We did exactly like she said and, sure enough, we heard the buttons whirring. We kept moving our hands in and out, in and out. When I looked at Ida Claire, she was grinning from ear to ear. And each of our buttons was humming on that string.

Grandmama told us that she had been saving something else for us that we might could use. She went back to her pantry to put up the ball of string and her scissors. When she came out, she had a square-looking brown cardboard box. When she sat it down on the floor, it came up as high as her knees. The box was empty. In the other hand she had a brown sack. When she shook it, something made a rattling sound. She emptied the sack out on the table. Shoot, there were more bottle caps than I had ever seen. "What can we do with those, Grandmama?" I asked her. She told us that they could be used in a checkers game. Ida Claire said that we didn't have a checkerboard. But Grandmama told her that that was what the box was going to be used to make.

She opened a little drawer of her sewing machine cabinet and pulled out a red and a black crayon. She also got a ruler and a pencil from another drawer. She told us to turn the box upside down and then the bottom of the box would be the top for the checkerboard. She showed us how to draw off the blocks on the box. It turned out to be a square. We drew eight different rows of eight blocks each. We had seen a checkers game before, we just didn't own one. Now, Grandmama gave us each a crayon. We got busy coloring the blocks. One was red and the next was black. While we were coloring, Grandmama got out her thread and started crocheting. She could really make that little silver needle move fast. I watched Ida Claire do it one time. But, all Grandmama had taught her how to do was the chain stitch. Ida Claire said that that kind of crocheting was easy. I thought that it should have been because all it looked like to me was a little bit fatter and longer thread. Ida Claire said that I could probably do it, too. But, I told her that I didn't want to. I knew that sewing stuff was sissy.

We heard a knock at the back screened door. We looked up and saw Millie with her face pressed against the door. She asked, "Is anybody home? What are y'all doing?"

Grandmama told Millie to come in. Ida Claire asked her, "How did you know where we were?" Millie told us that she saw our ball and gloves on the back porch. Then, Grandmama asked her if she wanted some tea cakes. While Millie was eating her tea cakes, we finished coloring the checkerboard. Ida Claire took twelve bottle caps and gave me twelve. She asked if I wanted mine turned upside down or right side up. I told her that it didn't matter to me. All the up-and-down-side talk was getting me confused.

Millie and Grandmama watched while I made the first move of the checkers game. Grandmama said, "I really do like your name, Millie. It fits you to a tea. Is it short for another name?"

Millie answered, "Yes, ma'am, it's my nickname. I'm really named after my Daddy's Mama. Her name was Millana. But, my Mama said that that was too much name for such a tiny baby, so she shortened it to Millie."

I asked Millie if she knew how Ida Claire got her name. She said that she didn't. Then she asked Ida Claire if she was named for anybody. Ida Claire said, "Grandmama, you tell her the story. You can explain it better than I can." We had quit playing checkers by this time.

So Grandmama began explaining to Millie how Ida Claire got her name. "It really was a combination of two people that made Ida Claire's name possible. Franklin was five years old when Ida Claire was born. The next day after the baby was born, Ben took Franklin and me to the hospital to visit with Ima and the new baby. She didn't have a name yet. When it came time to look in the window at her, Franklin and I both got to see the baby at the same time. As soon as I saw her, I thought that she was the prettiest little girl that I had ever seen. So, I said, 'Well, I declare, she is a pretty baby! What do you think, Franklin?' And, he said that he thought she was all right, for a girl. When we went back into Ima's room, she asked Franklin if he knew a good name for his new little sister. He told his Mama that he thought Grandmama had named her already. Ima looked at him sorta funny and asked him what he meant. And he said, 'Well, when Grandmama saw her, she said, "Ida Claire"! So, I think that's a good name for her.'"

Millie looked at Ida Claire and me. Then, she laughed. I was grinning because I had heard that story before. Then, I told Millie that Franklin said if he had had a chance he would have named me, too. He said that he would have told Aunt Sophie that they should have the letter "N" as my middle initial. Then my name would be Will N. Lee. He thought that would be a perfect name for me. He said that I "willingly" do whatever anybody asks. Millie laughed again and said, "Well, Will, I reckon that means you're always a pretty good sport."

And I said, "Yeah, I reckon so!" Ida Claire and Grandmama both nodded.

Chapter 19

Memory Lane Can Be A Mighty Wide Road

"Three more days of summer, Will. That's all we have left." Ida Claire said as she came in the kitchen door the next day. I was eating a tomato sandwich for dinner. She had a skate key tied on a shoelace that was hanging around her neck. And she had a skate in each hand. She asked, "Do you want to roller skate as soon as you get through eating?"

I told her, "Shoot, yeah. Let me get some socks and my cowboy boots." That little metal side piece had to be tightened so it would stay on good. So, I had to have some hard shoes on my feet. We went in the alley towards Dewey's house. Beside his house was the sidewalk. That's where we could roller skate. Ida Claire thought we might could use a rope while we were roller skating. She ran back to get it. I was fastening my last skate when she came back and plopped the rope on the ground. Ida Claire got her skates on in a hurry.

We started skating holding hands side by side. I hadn't been skating long, but I could do pretty good as long as I didn't have to make any quick turns. We used the rope to tie around our waists and pull each other. That would help the person in the back go even faster.

Aunt Ima called out the back door for Ida Claire to come there. So, both of us skated to the end of the sidewalk and walked on our skates to Ida Claire's house. Aunt Ima gave Ida Claire a dollar bill and told her to go to Mr. Gore's store and get some bread and milk. She said that we each could use a dime of the change that was left. So we sat on the back doorsteps and pulled off our skates. Ida Claire wrapped the shoelace skate key necklace around her skates. Then we went down the street to Mr.

Gore's store. All the way there Ida Claire kept saying, "Bread and milk, bread and milk, bread and milk." I reckon she wanted to be sure to remember what to buy. After she got the bread and milk, she put them up on the counter next to the cash register. Then she said, "Will, what do you want with your dime?" I was already at the ice cream freezer chest. I told her that I thought I wanted a banana Popsicle. Ida Claire said that she might want a Dreamsicle. Then, she said that she thought she would rather have a coca-cola and a bag of Chee-tos. I told her that I would get a coke, too. Ida Claire said, "That sounds good. We'll each have a coke to drink and I'll give you some Chee-tos if you want some." I told her that I could break my Popsicle in half and she could have half of it. We told Mr. Gore bye. And we got everything and headed home.

Ida Claire gave Aunt Ima the change and the sack with the bread and milk in it. We used the bottle opener to pop the bottle caps off our cokes. We went to the front porch to sit in the shade on the cool concrete steps. I broke the Popsicle down the middle and gave Ida Claire her half. We tried to eat it in a hurry so it wouldn't drip. If that Popsicle juice dripped down your hand, the gnats would just about worry you to death. Then, Ida Claire asked, "What's on the bottom of your coke bottle, Will?" We both raised the bottles above our heads to read the name of the town where they were made. Ida Claire read the name on her bottle very slowly. "Mine says 'Pe - o - ri - a. Ill.' I wonder where that is. What are your letters, Will?" I told her the letters on my bottle were T-A-M-P-A, F-L-A. Ida Claire said, "I wonder which one is farthest away. We'll have to ask Franklin to see which one of us wins."

We heard Uncle Ben come in the house. The afternoon sure had gone by fast. He was home from work already. We heard Aunt Ima say to him, "Your sister, Esther, called and wanted us to come eat supper with her tonight and visit." Uncle Ben told her that that sounded good to him.

Ida Claire leaned back on the front screened door and asked, "Mama, are we going to Aunt Esther's for supper? And can Will come?" Aunt Ima told her yes to both questions. I had met Aunt Esther before, but I had never been to her house. "Oh, boy, Will, you'll love going to Aunt Esther's house. She has the most stuff for you to look at, and she'll tell you anything you ask her about any of it. Daddy says that she is what's known as a collector. But the best thing about Aunt Esther is that she really likes to have children visit her. She always talks to me and Franklin just like we are as special as any grown-up she knows. And, you know, usually grown-ups like to just talk to other grown-ups. Since she saves everything, I'll bet she'll have some stuff that you never have seen before." By the time Ida Claire finished talking, I was really looking forward to going to Aunt Esther's house.

We drove up in Aunt Esther's driveway. She came out to the car and said, "Y'all get out. And, who do we have here? It's Will! I almost didn't recognize you because you've grown so big since I last saw you. I want all three of you good-looking children to come into this house." I could see what Ida Claire meant about Aunt Esther. I was feeling sorta special myself. We went into the living room. Aunt Esther said, "Y'all have a seat on the settee." She had two couches and lots of chairs in that big room. And, she had glassed-in shelves on every wall. They were all full, too. "Let me show y'all something that I bet you never have seen before." She left the room and then came back with something that was a little bit bigger than a football. It was a golden color and was shiny. When she got closer to us, we could tell it was a turtle's shell. She told us how she had fixed it so-o pretty. It really was different than a real turtle. Franklin said that that shellac made it nice and shiny.

After supper we went outside to sit. It was cooler outside in the night time breeze. There was a big street light on the corner of the street. There were a lot of frogs hopping around under that light. Franklin said that those frogs were eating the bugs from the light. He sure was smart! He asked us if we wanted to see how many frogs we could catch. I said, "Shoot, yeah!" Ida Claire nodded. Frogs always feel kinda gooshy when you squeeze 'em in the middle, but they're easy to catch.

Aunt Esther said, "I'll get some string for you." She laughed and then she said, "You've heard of walking your dogs, well, now you can say that you're walking your frogs." We all laughed. She gave us the string. Franklin, Ida Claire, and I each helped each other tie the string on the hind leg of each frog as we caught it. Then, we walked beside them as they jumped and walked along tied to the string. It sure was fun.

Aunt Ima said, "Esther, do you usually get the paper a day early? Ours comes tomorrow in the mail." Aunt Esther told her that she usually picked up a newspaper at the drugstore.

Then, Aunt Esther said, "Yep, as a matter of fact, I think I saw Ida Claire Loudly and Will Lee written in the paper. Let me show you."

Ida Claire said, "That's right, Will. We can find out who our teacher will be. The week that school starts the newspaper shows a list of the classes from first grade to third grade." Aunt Esther had opened the paper. Ida Claire and Franklin were both looking and reading. I would be glad when I could read, too. Ida Claire yelled, "Oh, boy, my teacher will be Mrs. Milton. That's who I wanted for third grade. And Millie will be in my class, too."

I asked Ida Claire if she saw my name yet. Franklin pointed to it and said, "I see it. Here it is. It says 'Squirt Lee'." I kinda wrinkled.

But Ida Claire said, "Don't worry, Will, Franklin is teasing you. Here it is - Will Lee -, and you're in Mrs. Dunn's first grade." She pointed her finger to the place on the paper that had my name. I did recognize it because Ida Claire had taught me how to spell it. I asked her if she knew Mrs. Dunn. She said, "She's great! She was my teacher when I was in first grade. She was Franklin's teacher, too."

Franklin said, "Yeah, you'll do good in her class because I broke her in just right for you!" And he grinned his sneaky grin.

I wasn't so sure about starting to school. I must have looked a little bit worried. Aunt Esther said to me, "You'll do great in school, Will. First grade is so much fun. And always remember, it's just as easy as lard is greasy!" I smiled and felt better. I knew that lard was mighty greasy. Ida Claire had been telling me for a long time that school was fun. Now, since a grown-up said it, too, I was about to believe it for sure.

On the way home that night, Franklin said, "It's funny to me how summertime goes by so-o fast. But when school starts, time goes by slow. It seems like Christmas time takes forever to get here." Aunt Ima said that the older you get, the faster time flies.

I whispered to Ida Claire that I was really getting scared about school starting. I didn't know if I'd be smart enough for first grade. She said to me that she believed I'd be the smartest one in my class. That made me feel better. Then she said, "Sometimes at night when I start wondering about things, I get scared, too. But then I like to think of what adventures we've had that day and all the fun we've had. And, you know, Will, even though summer is almost over, you can still remember all the fun stuff we did."

So the rest of the way home, I remembered some of the fun adventures we had during the summer. I thought about playing marbles and playing with the cardboard boxes from the shirt factory. I thought about playing with the peashooters and playing rock school. I thought about riding the sow and shooting off firecrackers. I thought about the Bible drill and I thought about making the tree house. I thought about playing cowboys and I thought about climbing in our favorite mimosa tree. I smiled and looked at Ida Claire. She must have been thinking the same things that I was. She smiled back and said, "We really had a great summer, didn't we, Will?" I nodded. And we both knew that we really were lucky!

THE END

To order books or schedule a school visit please contact Kay Heath at kayheath@mchsi.com 229-894-1711

Ida Claire, It's Summertime! $10.00 includes tax

Ida Claire, That's Funny! $10.00 includes tax

Ida Claire, That's A Mystery! $10.00 includes tax

Three Little Frogs in a Boomerang Journey $16.00 includes tax

Three Little Frogs Go to the Beach $16.00 includes tax

S&H cost $1-$25 is $4.00
$25 plus is $8.00

www.KayHeathBooks.com

Kay's books are available online and may be purchased via credit card at: Georgia SouthWestern State University Campus Bookstore.